ALSO BY GORDON KORMAN

Pop
Ungifted
Masterminds
Masterminds: Criminal Destiny
Masterminds: Payback
Supergifted
The Unteachables
Notorious
Unplugged

OPERATION DO-OVER

OPERATION DO-OVER

GORDON KORMAN

BALZER + BRAY

An Imprint of HarperCollins*Publishers*

Library of Congress Control Number: 2021941315
ISBN 978-0-06-303274-3

Typography by Erin Fitzsimmons
21 22 23 24 25 PC/LSCH 10 9 8 7 6 5 4 3 2 1

First Edition

*For Shari, "The Shopper," with
undying thanks!*

TWELVE YEARS OLD
OCTOBER 28

'm standing next to the bumper cars when the first bolt of lightning splits the sky and strikes the main transformer. The explosion is like a bomb blast.

I almost jump out of my skin.

Oh, man, I didn't even want to come to Harvest Festival, and now I'm going to get fricasseed before my thirteenth birthday!

A blinding shower of sparks rains down on the crowded fairgrounds as the lights blink once and wink out. The honky-tonk music from a dozen different rides and games suddenly stops as the bumper cars grind to a halt. A new sound rises—screams, howls of protest, crying babies, shouts of alarm from people stranded at the top of the Ferris wheel. It's like somebody flipped a switch, sending the fair from fun mode to full freak-out in the blink of an eye.

The storm comes out of nowhere. Just a few minutes ago, the sky was full of stars. Now it's pitch black, hard to see your hand in front of your face. A howling wind rakes the midway. We get pelted with a barrage of flying dust and litter—ride tickets, napkins, wrappers, paper cups, and straws.

You try to be a good kid—do your homework. Follow the rules. And what do you get for it? Blown away.

Something slams into the back of my head, nearly knocking me over. I wheel, expecting to see a cannonball—surely nothing less than that would pack such a punch. Smiling up at me from the ground is a pink teddy bear that must have sailed away from one of the game stalls. I reach for it, but the next gust of wind sends it tumbling away, where it's stomped to shreds by many fleeing feet.

Where does everybody think they're going? There's nowhere to go!

People are running—most for the exits, but some just because running is what you do in an emergency. I catch glimpses of faces I recognize—kids from my grade—

But where is *she*?

She's the only reason I'm here, even though she's the reason I should be a million miles away.

I want to call out to somebody, but what could I say, and who would hear me in this commotion? Flailing legs trip each other up, and bodies go down. That's when the rain comes in, sweeping across the midway. Pelting rain. The water causes the damaged transformer to burst into flames, casting an orange glow over the pandemonium.

Desperately, I fight through the panicked crowd, escaping behind a hot-dog stand. There I'm almost knee-deep in scattered buns, but at least I can breathe, free of the crush of people. Wires and cables swing dangerously overhead, sparks spurting from every connection.

I wipe the rain from my eyes, noting that not even all that water can soften my bristly stick-up hairline. Story of my life.

"Mason?" comes a plea, faint in the howling wind and pounding rain.

I'd know that voice anywhere. I've been half dreading it, half hoping to hear it since I got to the fairgrounds.

I squint into the gloom. Ava Petrakis stands at the base of the Tilt-A-Whirl, her drenched auburn hair plastered to her scalp, hugging her light jacket around her.

I run to her underneath the big ride. "It's okay! This can't last long!"

She looks like a half-drowned kitten. In spite of the wildness of the storm and the danger all around, my first thought is that the two of us have never been alone together before this moment. Was it really only a month ago that Ms. Alexander introduced the new girl to our seventh-grade class?

With a deafening crunch, a blast of wind tears the sign off the top of the Tilt-A-Whirl. For an instant, the heavy metal square twirls above our heads like a piece of scrap paper.

We watch it with terrified eyes. You don't have to be a science kid to know the law of gravity: What goes up must come down.

2

ZERO YEARS OLD

Mason Rolle and Tyrus Ehrlich get born.

I don't actually remember this, because I was zero at the time. But Ty and I are born just a couple of months apart—me first. And even though our families don't know each other very well, he and I are destined to become the greatest friends in the history of humanity.

I'm the only three-year-old at Gymboree who's too uncoordinated to figure out how to bounce a ball. At least, I am until Ty shows up. Compared to him, I'm LeBron James.

We're not best friends—not yet. At three, you're lucky if Pull-Ups are fully in your rearview mirror. It's more like we're *aware* of each other. When Ty face-plants on the playground, I cry. And when I get a nosebleed, Ty panics. Even though the word *friend* isn't in either of our vocabularies yet, the two of us have a sense: We're in this together.

At the sandbox tea party, we're the only two who get so into the game that we forget what we're doing and accidentally drink sand. That gets our moms acquainted—they're the ones who have to come into preschool to wash our mouths out. At make-believe we have no equal. It's in the physical world that the problems start. But it's okay, because there's always this other kid who's just as awful as you.

As we get older, this recurring problem in our lives starts to have a name: sports. We're bad at them. At tag, we're not fast enough to catch anyone, so we're doomed to be It forever. In musical chairs, we're the ones left standing. In T-ball, the bat flies out of our hands and conks somebody. At duck-duck-goose, we're total turkeys. And don't even get me started on dodgeball.

But as terrible as we are at sports, there are these

other games that we seem to be really good at. Like Monopoly, where both of us can make change in our heads, even for the really big amounts. And chess, where we're the only kids our age who can figure out how all the different pieces move.

I can't remember how old I am the first time I hear the word *nerd*. But once I hear it, I hear it a lot. And although I know it's meant as an insult, I'm kind of into it. I like the things that nerds like—science-y stuff, puzzles that make you think, shows and video games where characters fly through space, or travel through time. And it isn't lost on me that there's only one other kid in Pasco who hears the word *nerd* every bit as often as I do. Ty.

All this is leading up to the day in first grade when our class goes to the planetarium. It's the first field trip I remember that isn't all about things I'm bad at. I don't have to scale a climbing wall or follow a compass through some swamp or make it over a rope bridge. I just have to lean back, look at the stars, and dream. It's paradise. I wish it could last forever.

Afterward, there's a kid up at the front, and he's giving the curator a hard time. It's Ty—which seems weird, because if there's one person who should love this field trip, it's him.

Ty's really heated, practically in tears. So I lean in to listen.

"What do you mean, Pluto's not allowed to be a planet anymore? Of course it's a planet—it's my favorite one!"

It hits me then: What are the odds that two kids on the same little street of the same little town are both going to have a favorite planet? Mine happens to be Jupiter, because go big or go home. Still, it doesn't matter which planet we choose. It's the fact that we both chose one.

That's the moment—right then. Not only do we become best friends, but it dawns on both of us that we've already *been* best friends for years.

"We're not just friends—we're old friends," I decide.

"Either that or we went from zero to light speed in negative time," Ty adds smugly.

I grin, because I was about to say exactly the same thing.

Oh, sure, lots of people have a close friend, a BFF, a brother-from-another-mother. This is different. Ty and I share a two-brain hive mind. We finish each other's sentences. Sometimes we don't even have to do that, since our thoughts are identical anyway. We can look at each other and crack up laughing at a joke neither of us has to say out loud. Our parents think it's spooky.

We read the same books, watch the same shows, and play the same video games, usually together. If one of us gets grounded, the other one sits it out too, because what's the point of doing anything without your other half?

In second grade, we get put in two different classes. We survive less than three days. That's when the principal shows up to explain that there's been a computer glitch, and I get moved over to rejoin Ty. Yeah, right. That glitch turns out to be our folks not being able to deal with the nonstop nagging we've been giving them at home.

"This whole place would have to shut down if the Einstein twins couldn't be in class together," is the complaint from Dominic Holyoke, star athlete, big mouth, and slab of meat extraordinaire.

"The Dominator" is not our biggest fan. To be honest, we're not that popular at Pasco Elementary School—or at Pasco Middle School after that. We're not unpopular either. We're just nobody. And that suits us fine. To each other, we're everybody that matters.

We roll into seventh grade at the top of our game, as defending science-fair champions and cofounders of the astronomy club. We've got Ms. Alexander—our favorite teacher—for homeroom, but it isn't all perfection. Dominic is in the class too, and so is his sidekick, Miggy Vincent, master of spitballs and smart-alecky comments. I'm extra vulnerable to spitballs. I have this front section of bristly stick-up hair that catches them like a basket.

A classic Dominic and Miggy stunt: One September morning, I flop into my seat at the front table and find myself superglued to the chair. I stand up again quickly and the chair comes with me. I try to pull myself free. No dice. My jeans are totally bonded to the wood.

It isn't hard to identify the source of this prank. Partway across the room, those two boneheads are practically smothering themselves to keep from laughing out loud.

Without a word, Ty takes in the situation, walks calmly to the art supply closet, and comes back with a paintbrush and a container of nail polish remover that we use as a solvent. Dominic and Miggy watch in growing annoyance as he soaks the brush and works to free the seat of my pants. Within a few minutes, I'm up on my feet, rescued.

"Because . . . science." I beam at the two culprits

while Ty uses the nail polish remover to clean the rest of the superglue off my chair.

"Shut up, Spaceman," Dominic grumbles. His latest nickname for me—one that's destined to last a long time.

That's the power of the greatest friendship in human history. Ty and I may not be cool. But we've got each other's backs one thousand percent. Plus, we're smart, so it's hard to imagine that there's anything middle school could throw at us that we can't handle.

At that moment, Ms. Alexander walks into the class, leading a petite girl with a heart-shaped face, blue-green eyes, and a silky cascade of auburn hair.

"We have a new student in our homeroom. Class, this is Ava Petrakis, who comes to us from New York City. Let's all do our best to make her feel welcome."

3

SEVENTEEN YEARS OLD

My reflection looks distorted in the smeared and speckled mirror of the high school bathroom.

I run some water over my hand and try to smooth the section of hair that sticks up at the top of my forehead. No amount of combing, brushing, gelling, or styling will convince that tuft to lie down or sweep to the side. It's better than it was in middle school, when the buzz cut Mom made me get only encouraged it to stand up straighter, like the bristles of a stiff brush. At least now, at seventeen, I'm in charge of my own hairstyle. If I keep growing it—in theory—at some point the force of gravity has to take over, and it will all lie down beautifully. As an A-plus science student, I have a lot of faith in physics. Newton explained it perfectly: I just need the downward pull of gravity to be stronger than the upward push of the tuft. At this moment, it seems like the tuft will have to reach halfway to Alpha Centauri before gravity gains the upper hand. It's definitely not going to happen now, in the passing period between fourth and fifth hour.

I step out of the bathroom and wade into the hustle of kids on their way to the next class. At Pasco High School, if you're not moving fast enough when you join the procession, you get trampled.

"Hi, Mason!" Clarisse Ostrov accelerates the motion of her long, gangly legs to match my pace. "Have you signed up for the planetarium trip yet?" She has a way of looking at me through her Coke-bottle glasses that makes me feel like I'm a lab specimen being examined under a microscope. "Better hurry," she adds without waiting for my answer. "Once the bus fills up, they won't take anybody else."

"Oh, right," I say sarcastically, indicating the crowd

surging around us. "Nothing but planetarium fans as as far the eye can see."

A stray elbow comes out of nowhere, nearly catapulting me into the lockers. "Out of the way, Spaceman."

"Jerk!" Clarisse exclaims, waving her skinny arms at the class-change parade. She comes over to me. "Sorry, I didn't see who it was."

I shrug. It's not hard to guess. Dominic or maybe Miggy, my tormentors from way back. Spaceman is the nickname they gave me in middle school, thanks to my status as cofounder of the astronomy club. Clarisse was one of our first members. She knows as well as anybody that both those jerks have been on my case pretty much nonstop since then. Probably my own fault for starting a club about planets, stars, and galaxies. I guess I could have created a gardening group, but I didn't want to be Fertilizer Face. Or worse.

"I'm okay," I tell her.

"Sign up for the trip," she says again. "Don't get left out." And she strides off.

I heave a sigh. Liking astronomy is nothing to be ashamed of, no matter what the Dominics and Miggys of the world think. Might as well head to the science office and sign up. Otherwise, Clarisse will never let me hear the end of it. Our local planetarium isn't exactly the Mauna Kea Observatory in Hawaii, but don't knock it. I love planetariums—ever since that first-grade trip. I had birthday parties there when I was little.

I poke my head in through the doorway. And freeze.

There's only one person at the sign-up sheet—the other cofounder of the astronomy club at Pasco Middle School: Ty. And that means there's no way I can go.

The disappointment is bitter on my tongue as I wheel and walk away. The class-change crowd has thinned out now, so I'm partway down the hall when Mrs. Nekomis catches up to me.

"Where are you going, Mason? You haven't signed up yet!"

"I can't go," I lie. "I have a doctor's appointment."

"You do not!" she exclaims. "This is about Ty, isn't it? He's going, so you won't."

I don't even bother giving her an argument. Mrs. Nekomis knows better than anybody how it is with Ty and me. She was our seventh-grade homeroom teacher back when it all happened—Ms. Alexander in those days.

"It was five years ago, Mason," she pleads. "Don't you think it's time for both of you to put it behind you? You were children back then. You'll be going to college soon. You were such wonderful, close friends. How can you throw all that away?"

I stare at her, my face hardening to stone. She's a hundred percent right. Ty and I *were* close. That's the whole problem. The two of us had been best friends ever since Gymboree. No—the word *friends* doesn't come close to describing what we had. We were *synced*, like two devices on the same identity. Each of our families understood that it had adopted an extra son.

Until Ava came.

It wasn't her fault. That's the one thing Ty and I still agree on. And when Ava realized what had happened because of her, she was totally devastated. Even now, five years later, she walks on eggshells around us for fear of doing any more damage.

But the damage is done. That's what Mrs. Nekomis can never understand. When you've been that close to someone, and your friendship is ripped apart, it leaves an open wound that can never heal. And just seeing that person—even on a planetarium trip—is unbearable. When I look at Ty, he's more than some kid I used to hang out with way back when. I feel the loss of everything we had and everything we were ever going to have. It's been five years, and it hasn't gotten better.

And it never will.

TWELVE YEARS OLD
SEPTEMBER 27

Ava's arrival is like four thousand volts of electricity shot through the walls of Ms. Alexander's homeroom.

In the front row, I lean over to Ty at precisely the moment he leans over to me—and naturally, our eyebrows are raised at the exact same angle. Nothing new ever happens in a dinky town like Pasco. I mean, we started kindergarten with a lot of the same kids in this very class. So Ava might as well have the word *New* written across her forehead in chaser lights.

But even more than that, the girl has something. What is it? Style? Her clothes are pretty much the same as what everybody else is wearing. Maybe it's just the way she's wearing them. She's got attitude, for sure. Here she is, the newbie, but there isn't an ounce of shyness to her. It's like she instantly belongs wherever she is—including here.

"How many times did you get mugged in New York?" Miggy pipes up. Typical him.

"Never," Ava replies without missing a beat.

Ms. Alexander frowns at Miggy. "That's not a very polite question."

"It's fine," Ava says airily. "A lot of people think New York is dangerous. But you just have to put out a vibe that you don't want to be messed with, and nobody messes with you."

She has everybody's attention now. Pasco isn't exactly the boonies, but no one around here says anything like that. Ava is *different*.

Even Ms. Alexander is impressed. "Well, find a seat, Ava. We have a few things to take care of before first period."

An odd tension rises in the room as Ava surveys the open spots. Suddenly it seems very important where the new girl will choose to sit.

Ty and I crane our necks to see where she'll go. My money is on the empty seat in the cluster of desks where Miggy and Dominic hold court. They're the big sports stars, so a lot of kids gravitate toward them. But in a rare disagreement with me, Ty seems to be looking over at a vacancy by the window, near Emma, Kennedy, and a few of the other popular girls—the ones who have the most Instagram followers, and who dominate the seventh-grade chat.

So many choices. Where is Ava from New York going to land?

Everybody's so focused on the drama that I'm surprised by the scraping of the chair as Ava sits down at the table we share with Clarisse.

Ava beams at the three of us. "This seat taken?"

Ty and I are struck dumb. I don't think he heard the question.

"I'm Clarisse," Clarisse introduces herself from behind her large, thick glasses. "And these two lunkheads are Mason and Ty. Believe it or not, they know how to talk. Sometimes."

"Hi, Clarisse. Hi, guys."

"We talk!" Ty and I exclaim in such perfect unison that the whole class laughs. Sometimes there are drawbacks to being on the same wavelength as your best friend.

It shouldn't be a problem that Ava's sitting with us. But to be honest, I'm so extra aware of her that I spend all of homeroom in stiff-necked misery, forcing my total focus onto the teacher. Out of the corner of my eye, I can see Ty doing the same thing. To make matters worse, Dominic and Miggy bombard us with spitballs the entire time. Yikes—I feel one of them catch in the mini basket formed by my stick-up hair, but I don't dare flick it away. What if Ava notices?

When the bell finally releases us to first period, Ty and I can't get out of there fast enough.

"What do you think of Ava?" he asks on the way to the science lab.

"She's . . . nice."

"Nice," Ty confirms. "Yeah, I thought so too."

Funny—the two of us can go on for hours about any subject—video games, sunspots, Chipotle versus Five Guys, robots, does Batman count as a real superhero, toast, and our absolute favorite topic: time travel. But on the subject of Ava Petrakis, we can come up with exactly one word between the two of us: *nice*.

In the lab, we're waiting for the okay to begin the experiment when Ava appears in the doorway.

"Sorry I'm late," she greets Mr. Esposito, handing over her course card. "The room numbering in this school is totally confusing. I almost ended up in a closet."

The teacher nods. "Everyone else has a partner, so you'll just have to find one of the pairs to work with for the time being."

"Pull up over here," Dominic invites.

"Yeah," Miggy adds. "Treat yourself to a free upgrade."

Once again, the girl from New York marches right past them and establishes herself on the stool between Ty and me. "Hi, guys. Miss me?"

Going by the flush in Ty's cheeks, I can only imagine my own beet-red complexion. The two of us nearly conk heads stooping to make room for her book bag. This time there's no question about it. She's *choosing* us. On *purpose*.

Ava lights the Bunsen burner with an authoritative flick of the flint and has a beaker of solution heating over it in no time at all. "I'm kind of a science dweeb," she explains, grinning.

"No way!" Ty blurts.

"Us too!" I add. "I mean, not *too* dweeby—"

"There's no such thing as too dweeby," she lectures.

"Never apologize for being smart. Hey, you got something in your hair," she adds, flicking the spitball out of my bristles.

We regard her with a new respect. We've always gotten great grades, but it was kind of understood that there was a price to be paid in the coolness department for being good at school. We even developed an equation for it: $P=1/GPA$—meaning that your popularity is inversely proportional to your grade point average. Yet here's Ava from New York, and she doesn't believe in $P=1/GPA$ at all. She thinks being smart is fine. Better still, she *is* smart! She runs through the experiment with such ease and authority that all we can do is watch in awed silence.

Later, in the cafeteria, I'm carrying my lunch to the usually solitary table I share with Ty, when a chair is suddenly kicked into my path. In an amazing display of body control, I manage to keep my balance, but a hard-boiled egg rolls off my tray, landing with a crack on the tile floor and lying in a circle of shattered shell.

When I bend down to clean up the mess, Dominic is glaring into my face.

"Listen, Spaceman. I know what you're doing and you can forget it."

"Doing?" I'm mystified. "I'm not doing anything."

"If you two losers think you've got first dibs on the new girl, you're bugging," Miggy puts in. "It's one thing that she sits with you in homeroom because maybe she's nearsighted and can't see the normal people. But the cafeteria isn't school. It's real life."

I take stock of their long table, which is in the best location in the whole lunchroom—central, but just out of the glare of the large windows and not too close to the food line. It hosts a Who's Who of the seventh grade—athletes and cheerleaders and even a couple of eighth graders.

I shrug. "Ava sits wherever she wants."

"Right," Dominic agrees. "And she wants to sit here. Now scram."

As I start away, Dominic punches the bottom of my tray, and I lose a plastic fork and a small fruit cup. It's worth it to get clear of those mouth-breathers.

"What was that all about?" Ty asks when I join him, making sure to take the seat facing away from Dominic and Miggy's table.

"It's a long story," I grunt.

A few minutes later, Ava's voice rings out in the cafeteria. "Oh, that's okay. I'm sitting with friends."

Ty's eyes glaze over.

"She's coming this way, isn't she?"

He can only nod.

And then she's upon us, and the conversation begins even before she takes her first bite. "This food is way more basic than my old cafeteria in New York. We had a sushi bar . . ."

Lunch periods at Pasco Middle School are an inhuman twenty-four minutes, but that's more than enough time for Ava Petrakis to share her entire life story. Her old apartment in New York was less than three blocks from the Museum of Natural History; she likes *Star Wars* better than *Star Trek*, but only because the transporter is "problematic from a science standpoint"; her Xbox Live gamer handle is Darth Hamster; her mom is a molecular biologist who is sequencing the genome of a kumquat; and if a genie ever grants her three wishes, the first one will be to go back in time to meet the Danish astronomer Tycho Brahe and see if he really had a silver nose.

I'm wide-eyed. "What about the second and third wishes?"

"I haven't worked that out yet," she admits. "Don't rush me. I might not even need the genie. Time travel isn't as impossible as it sounds. Do you know that the astronauts who travel to the International Space Station come back a tiny bit younger than they would be if they'd stayed on Earth?"

It's that very moment—when the words *time travel* pass her lips—when it hits me: I've just met the most awesome girl who has ever lived. Seriously, she's interesting; she's smart; she's nice; she likes time travel. She's still talking, but I'm not hearing anymore. I'm thinking, what are the odds that, of all the schools in all the towns, Ava would come here? What are the odds that she would be placed in my homeroom and choose to attach herself to me?

And Ty, I remind myself, noticing him across the table. And because I can read Ty's mind as easily as my own, I know exactly what he's thinking.

Which is: *I've just met the most awesome girl who has ever lived.*

TWELVE YEARS OLD
OCTOBER 12

By the time Ava has been in Pasco for a couple of weeks, it's hard to imagine a time when she wasn't there. She's a mainstay at our table at lunch, our astronomy club after school, and our Fortnite and Halo battles online. She's in class with Ty and/or me for seven of the eight daily periods. Homework is rarely done without the three of us together. Ava is plowing through our favorite books, TV shows, and movies at a record pace, and we—a little more slowly—are picking up on her interests, including Tycho Brahe, the guy with the silver nose. We even agree to combine on a science-fair project this year—the first time Ty and I have ever included an outsider. The topic: What else? Time travel.

"Really?" Clarisse whispers in the Spanish room. "Last year, when I wanted to work with you guys, you said no third wheels."

Spanish is our only class without Ava, who takes French.

"Mason and I are always a team," Ty explains. "You know that."

"And we won first prize," I remind her.

"So why Ava this year?" Clarisse persists. "Isn't she a third wheel?"

"Of course not," Ty replies. "The whole thing was her suggestion. Obviously, we can't build a time machine as a working model, so we're going to focus on examples in science when time gets distorted, like around black holes."

"Ava's idea," I add.

"I have ideas, too, you know," she says icily.

"You're great at science," Ty agrees. "I'll bet you'll take second place again. After us and Ava."

"In your dreams," Clarisse shoots back.

"I have great dreams," Ty informs her. "They're exactly like reality."

Those two go back and forth at each other forever sometimes. Neither one of them can resist having the last word.

Clarisse runs her hands through her curly, dark hair and comes up smiling just a little too sweetly. "So which one of you guys is dating her?"

"Nobody is," I tell her in surprise. "We're just friends."

"And science-fair partners," Ty chimes in. "Why would you ask that?"

"Open your eyes," Clarisse says sharply. "Seventh grade is all about who's dating who. Kennedy is dating Miggy. Emma used to go out with DeShaun, and now she's with Dominic. Gabriella broke up with Jake, but they're getting back together again. So which of you is with Ava?"

Ty blurts, "It's not like that —"

"*En español, por favor!*" Señora Kaufman's rule is that all conversation in her class must be in Spanish. No exceptions. "You can stand in the hall until you're ready to show your fellow students some courtesy!"

"Way to go, Clarisse!" I mutter as soon as the door

closes behind us. "Now Señora Kaufman hates us!"

"And for what?" Ty adds. "A conversation about nothing."

Clarisse sighs. "I guess it's for the best that neither of you guys has the guts to date Ava."

"Yeah," I confirm. Then, "Wait—why?"

"Isn't it obvious? If one of you ends up with her, there's no way whoever gets left out is going to be mature enough to handle it. It'll be like the end of the world."

"Not mature?" Ty crows. "Who's more mature than me? I lost all my Halo coins in a power failure, and I didn't even call tech support. I sucked it up and started again from zero."

"You're an animal," I assure him with a fist bump.

"It's not the same kind of mature," Clarisse points out, rolling her eyes.

"Nobody's dating anybody," Ty informs her evenly. "Ava is just one of the guys."

But the next time I see Ava, just outside math class, I have to admit that "one of the guys" is the last description I'd apply to her. She smiles, and I feel it in my liver. Then I remember that she's smiling at Ty too. Not only that, but Ty steps back to allow her to enter the doorway first. What's that supposed to mean?

Clarisse's words come back to me: *If one of you ends up with her . . .*

I shake myself—almost like Rufus, my English sheep-dog, when he comes out of the water at the beach.

Get a grip.

We take our usual seats on either side of her. All through the class, I look straight ahead at Mr. Sorenson while peering at Ava out of the corner of my eye. And what do I see? Ty, peering out of the corner of *his* eye at Ava.

After school, we walk Ava partway home as always. She's her usual bubbly self. It never ceases to amaze me how many topics she can bring up during a fifteen-minute walk. Today it's:

1) Possible backgrounds for the display board of our time-travel project;

2) How many Chinese restaurants were within half a mile of her old apartment in New York City (seven);

3) What purpose in nature is served by parsley, when it has no taste and no nutritional value; and

4) What happened to Tycho Brahe's original nose that he had to get a silver one? (It got cut off in a duel, which proves that not all science nerds are boring.)

We drop her off and head for our part of the neigh-borhood.

"What are you up to tonight?" I ask Ty before start-ing for my own door.

"Nothing."

Ty says that pretty much every day. How come today it sounds like a lie? Nobody can do literally *nothing*. Everything is something—fiddling with your phone, lying on the couch, watching Netflix, maybe even . . . sneaking over to Ava's place *without your best friend*.

"It's like you're a million miles away, Mason," my mother comments at dinner. "Did something happen at school today?"

"Maybe Mason's got a girlfriend," my nine-year-old sister, Serena, suggests in a singsong voice, lisping past her palate expander.

I start. "What? Why would you think that?"

"I don't," she replies. "No girl could ever be desper-ate enough."

"Serena," my father warns.

After dinner, I take Rufus out into the garage for our nightly routine. The sheepdog is so hairy that he has to be regularly vacuumed with an industrial-strength Shop-Vac, or he'll leave clumps of fur all over the house. I know it sounds like animal cruelty or something, but it's actually Rufus's favorite part of the whole day. When he sees other dogs being brushed or combed, he puffs up with pride, knowing that grooming for him is much more special and requires earsplittingly loud equipment and a fifty-foot extension cord.

But as Rufus rolls around on his back, exposing his underbelly to the Shop-Vac's brush attachment, I'm finding it impossible to focus. I just can't get the conversation with Clarisse out of my head.

What total garbage. Why should I listen to *her*? She doesn't know anything about Ava. She isn't even really friends with Ty and me. And yet, there's no denying that the stuff she said about the seventh grade is a hundred percent legit. All anybody wants to talk about is who's dating who, who broke up with who, and who dumped who for somebody else. So it makes sense that Clarisse might extend all that to include Ava, Ty, and me.

It *isn't* garbage. It just happens to be wrong.

Correction, I remind myself: It's wrong *so far*. After all, Kennedy and Miggy weren't together either—until they were. Now they spend all their spare time leaning against each other and everybody calls them

Miggennedy. No wonder I got suspicious when Ty said he was doing "nothing" tonight. Not that I *believe* the guy will sneak over to Ava's place, but because it's *possible*.

Rufus barks in confusion and more than a little impatience. Lost in thought, I've pulled the Shop-Vac's hose off the dog's belly, and I'm holding it up in the air. From Rufus's perspective, that is an unacceptable shirking of responsibility.

"Sorry." I flip the sheepdog over and start vacuuming his furry back. But my heart just isn't in it anymore. Somehow, when I wasn't looking, kids going out with each other became the new normal around here. And nobody kept Ty and me in the loop!

Unless—once again, the Shop-Vac ends up pointing at the ceiling—Ty has been in the loop this whole time. He's just not telling me because that gives him an advantage with Ava. How could my best friend be so devious? How could he be such a jerk? We have to have this out before it goes any further!

No sooner has that thought crossed my mind than the garage door begins to rise, and there stands Ty, silhouetted against the dusky sky. I shut off the Shop-Vac and quiet descends in the garage.

"We have to talk!" we chorus at exactly the same instant.

It lightens the mood and we smile at each other. Even at this moment of tension, our thoughts seem to be synchronized.

"I'll go first," Ty volunteers. "I've been thinking about what Clarisse said—about which one of us is going out with Ava."

"Which is *nobody*," I put in pointedly.

"Right! And remember she told us that no matter who it is, the other guy won't be able to handle it?"

"Baloney!" I exclaim. "Pure baloney!"

"On the annoying scale from one to ten, Clarisse is at least an eleven," Ty complains. "I was so ticked off!"

"Me too! I can't even vacuum my dog like a normal person!"

"I Photoshopped the Coalsack Nebula onto her sixth-grade picture and texted it to her. You know, like, *your brain is an interstellar dust cloud*. Good one, right?"

"Savage." I offer up my fist and we bump and slap through our secret handshake. "What did she have to say to that?"

"She called me a cretin. I googled it. Either it's an insult or she thinks I'm from this island called Crete. Only"—Ty's eyes drop to the toes of his sneakers—"I've been wondering whether she might be kind of a little bit right. Not about Crete. I mean about"—it's a struggle for him to speak the name—"Ava."

It's at that moment I realize what Ty has already figured out: Clarisse isn't just "a little bit right." She hit the nail on the head hard enough to drive it clear through the crust of the earth. Ty and I aren't immune to what's going on in the seventh grade. We're patients one and two in the epidemic! We both have a thing for Ava, and not a small thing either. From the instant she walked into Ms. Alexander's homeroom and chose to sit with us, we were doomed. And now no matter which of us she decides to go out with, it will shatter our friendship into such tiny pieces that not even the Shop-Vac will be able to gather them together.

My voice is barely a whisper. "What do we do?"

Ty's face is grave. "Romulans and Klingons."

Maybe no one else in the world would understand, but to me, it's perfectly clear. In *Star Trek*, the Romulans and the Klingons are enemy races. In order to avoid a war, both sides have to enter an agreement, promising not to attack the other.

"A treaty?" I ask.

Ty nods. "A non-Ava treaty. I mean, we can still be friends with her, but it never goes any further than that. It's like we told Clarisse—Ava's just one of the guys."

It's not the first moment I've reflected that I have the greatest best friend in the history of humanity. But this might be Ty's finest hour. It's the perfect solution. We're both crushing on Ava—strong word, but it's time to admit it's the truth. Sooner or later, she's bound to pick one of us, setting off a nuclear bomb in our friendship. The only way to avoid that is to eliminate the possibility for both of us at the same time, to put it permanently out of reach.

"A non-Ava treaty," I repeat, trying the idea on for size.

"If it worked for the Romulans and Klingons, it can work for us," Ty agrees.

"We should swear on it to seal the deal."

We look around. The garage is home to old paint cans, car supplies, rock salt, and an assortment of furnace filters and garden tools. There's nothing worthy of a solemn oath.

"We'll swear on Rufus," I decide. "He's loyal to the end, and that's what we'll be."

We each grasp the hose of the Shop-Vac and run the vacuum over Rufus's favorite spot—his left haunch. The big dog squirms with happiness. For him, it doesn't get any better than a double treatment.

TWELVE YEARS OLD
OCTOBER 19

Walking into Pasco Middle School with a secret treaty in my back pocket puts a spring in my step.

"What's the problem, Spaceman?" Dominic growls as I skip up the front stairs. "Forget to turn off your antigravity boots?"

I ignore him. I'm so happy with the way Ty and I handled our dilemma that not even Dominic's ragging can spoil my mood.

A good treaty can set you free. Yesterday, for example, Ava and Ty walked to school together while I was at the dentist. Before, that might have made me jealous. But now there's a treaty in place. And it's impossible to be jealous of something that can't happen.

The best thing about the non-Ava treaty is that it isn't non-Ava at all. The three of us are hanging out together more than ever, planning our science-fair project on time travel. Ava is now a full copresident of the astronomy club. Ty and I are plowing through the Hitchhiker's Guide to the Galaxy book series, which Ava recommended. And it's never far from our minds that Ava gravitated toward us even after Dominic, Miggy, and the popular kids made it more than clear that she was welcome to join their group.

"Mason—over here!"

Ava stands by my locker, waving and beckoning. Her T-shirt depicts a flying saucer attacking New York City, except it's actually a giant pepperoni pizza. Nobody else in Pasco would wear anything like that. The sun pouring through an overhead skylight turns her auburn hair to flame. That's another advantage of the treaty. I can admit to myself what a crush I have on her, and it's a hundred percent safe. The treaty covers all that—and covers it for Ty too.

"Follow me!" Ava grabs my hand and starts tugging me through the hall.

"What's going on?"

She pulls me into a stairwell, reaches into a small bag, and holds out a cookie. "Try this."

I take a bite and chew thoughtfully. "Really good, but it's peanut butter. Ty can't have this. He's allergic."

"I know. I brought them just for you. My grandma's specialty. Awesome, right?"

They are awesome—rich and peanutty, the kind of recipe that doesn't come from a mix, but only from people's grandmothers. It's a shame Ty can't—

All at once, the cookie turns to acid in my mouth. Ava knew about Ty's allergy. She brought these for me and me alone. Could this count as a treaty violation?

"What's the matter?" she asks. "Don't you like it?"

"Delicious," I tell her, almost gagging.

Well, obviously, there's a big difference between eating cookies and getting a girlfriend. The scary part is how easily a situation pops up between Ava and me that Ty can't be a part of. It doesn't break the treaty, but it shows how fragile an agreement like that can be. The Romulans and Klingons came close to destroying the whole galaxy half a dozen times over this kind of thing. Not peanut butter cookies, but some pretty minor stuff.

She holds out another. "Round two?"

"No, thanks. I'm on a diet."

The peanut butter cookies are just the beginning.

As the days pass, I start noticing things about Ava I haven't picked up on before.

For example, when Ty and I are sitting together in the cafeteria or in class, she always takes the seat on my side, not Ty's. And when the three of us are talking, she never looks at Ty. It's always at me.

At first, I thought it was all in my head. But when Ava Petrakis looks at you, you know you're being looked at. She has these huge blue-green eyes. It's like being hypnotized.

"Do you notice anything strange about Ava?" I ask Ty.

"Like what?"

He doesn't know. He has no idea. In Ty's mind, there has only ever been Ava and Mason and Ty. Yet now it seems like there's a separate grouping—Ava and Mason—lurking in the shadows.

"Nothing," I grumble. "I'm probably imagining it."

"Maybe it's a girl thing," Ty muses. "Nah, that can't be it. Ava's just one of the guys."

I try to laugh with him, but it comes out a sick gurgle. How is it possible that I'm feeling guilty for doing absolutely nothing? Am I supposed to confront Ava and demand equal eye contact time for Ty? She'll think I'm losing it!

Still, I *did* accept a giant Tupperware of those cookies, and I never told Ty. What would be the point? Ty couldn't eat them anyway.

The whole incident got me so stressed that I lost my appetite. Which turned out to be a bad thing, because Rufus scarfed down the entire cookie batch and part of the Tupperware lid too. The sheepdog spent the rest of the day throwing up. The Shop-Vac got a workout that night, that's for sure.

Lately, Ava has been talking a lot about Harvest Festival, which is a Pasco tradition every October. It's a typical fall fair, with tractor pulls and contests for the best pie and the fattest pig. You get the picture: hay rides, a corn maze, plus a haunted house, since the festival always runs through Halloween. There's a giant scale with a Mini Cooper on one side, and anyone who can grow a pumpkin that weighs more than the car wins it. The car, not the pumpkin.

Although most of the rides and games are targeted toward little kids, it's still kind of fun. But to hear Ava tell it, the Walt Disney Company is building their next great theme park in the middle of our town. Or maybe it's the dinkiness of Harvest Festival that appeals to her. She's used to big-city living in New York, so prize pigs and homemade jam sound exotic to her.

She's going on and on about how we have to make plans to go to the festival when it opens on Saturday night. And it slowly dawns on me: Ava blabs nonstop about the fair when it's just the two of us. But when Ty is around, she never brings up the subject at all.

Or could it be that's just how I see it? And when *I'm* not around, she's talking *Ty's* ears off about how excited she is for Saturday.

So I ask him a casual question: "Has Ava mentioned anything about Harvest Festival on Saturday?"

Ty seems surprised. "Harvest Festival? Ava? Like a city girl would waste her time at some small-town fall fair."

And I just know. The evidence has been mounting ever since cookie day, but there's no denying it anymore. The *we* Ava keeps mentioning is a twosome, not a threesome. It's happening just the way Clarisse predicted. She must be a witch, or have ESP or some-thing. Ava has chosen between us—and she picked *me*!

Good thing we had the brains to form the non-Ava treaty. Otherwise, Ty and I could be in real trouble here!

Only—for some reason, the treaty doesn't seem like the world's greatest idea anymore. Maybe it's this: When it was created, Ty and I each had a fifty percent probability of being the guy Ava chose and the guy she rejected. It made perfect sense to give up the chance to be her boyfriend in exchange for being spared the agony of ending up on the outside looking in.

But now my chances of the bad stuff have gone down to zero. Which means I traded going out with Ava—for *nothing*! If the Romulans or the Klingons had realized that they made such a terrible deal, they would have torn up their treaty in a heartbeat. But if I try to do that, Ty will never speak to me again, and he'll be right.

Our friendship is more important than anything. I could never risk that.

Knowing a girl likes you turns out to be the most nerve-racking thing I've ever had to deal with. The problem is that Ava is an almost permanent presence in my life. I see her constantly at school. And now that the three of us are working on the science-fair project together, she's in my face evenings and weekends too.

It's one thing to crush on a girl when it's all in your head and you know it's never going to turn into anything real. But when the girl is crushing on you back, and you can't make a move because of a *treaty*—a useless treaty you only joined because you have the brains of a mosquito—that really hurts.

Normally, when something's eating away at me, the person I talk it out with is Ty. Like how we figured out that hanging old CDs from the Ehrlichs' oak tree would chase away woodpeckers, and that Dad's microwave popcorn was the culprit for slowing down our Wi-Fi for online gaming. We saved an expensive visit to the vet when Ty suggested that Rufus's acid reflux was a nervous stomach from watching Serena's animal rescue shows on TV. But in this case, obviously, I have to be careful.

"Remember when we formed that non-Ava treaty?" I casually broach the subject with Ty. "You know— how dumb it was? We were real doofuses then."

Ty stares back with that frown that always wrinkles his nose. "What are you talking about? It was, like, ten days ago. And it's the smartest thing we ever did."

So much for that strategy. Now not only do I have to contend with the Ava situation; I have the extra added guilt of wishing that my best friend would move to Timbuktu or better still, Moon Base Alpha.

Later that day, Ava asks for the umpteenth time: "You're coming to Harvest Festival on Saturday, right?"

"I don't think I'm going to be able to make it." Just getting those words out is so painful that I probably look like I'm blowing a bowling ball through my left nostril.

"Why not?" she asks in a wounded tone.

That's the toughest question of all. How can you tell the girl of your dreams that you entered into a treaty that's all about avoiding her?

"I think I might have a thing that night."

"What thing?"

I shrug miserably. "It's—family stuff." Blame it on Mom and Dad.

Ava has to accept that. Surely, New York parents volunteer their kids for stuff they can't get out of too.

But on Thursday, she brings it up again. "What did your folks say?"

I'm blindsided. "About what?"

"The fair!" she exclaims. "Is your family thing still

on, or are you going to be able to come Saturday night?"

When I don't answer, her face fills with disappointment. "You didn't even bother to ask, did you?"

My mouth has gone so dry that I feel almost inside out. Never could I have imagined how awful it would be to let her down. I hate myself. I'm even mad at Ty, who has no idea any of this is happening. If there ever was a lose-lose situation, this is it.

A slap in the back of the head nearly knocks me flying. Dominic swaggers onto the scene, obnoxious as ever.

"You're never going to get a straight answer from Spaceman," he tells Ava. "His pea brain is out exploring Uranus."

Miggy sticks his nose into it. "If you actually want to have fun at Harvest Festival, come hang with us. Life's better with the cool people."

I feel the hair on the back of my neck standing at attention. "Actually, the family thing got canceled," I say to Ava, my tongue moving faster than my mind. "So I'm in. I'll catch up with you there."

TWELVE YEARS OLD
OCTOBER 28

Go home.

The fairgrounds are almost a mile from my house. Those two words circle my head all the way there. They prove that I know better than this.

Go home . . . Stay away. . . .

The non-Ava treaty hangs over me like that sword from Greek mythology. I can tell myself I'm not violating it: *Oh, I'm going to Harvest Festival and she happens to be there too. What's the big deal? I see her every day at school.*

So how come I didn't tell Ty about it? Even bring him along? We do everything else together. Why not this?

Because he's not the one she chose.

A treaty is a sacred oath. We vacuumed a dog over it. The Romulans and Klingons trusted the entire safety of the galaxy to a promise just like ours, and I can't even make it through a weekend.

I enter through the front gate and melt into the throng on the midway. Spinning rides, game stalls, blaring music, smells from a dozen different kinds of food. People milling everywhere.

See? She's not here. Now you can leave . . .

But I already know I have no intention of following my own advice. I'm a treaty-breaker, lower than low.

My brain is whirling with a million different thoughts—Ty, the treaty, Ava. It never even occurs to me to worry about the weather. It was a beautiful day changing into a beautiful night—starry skies, gentle breeze, a harvest moon. How can all that turn into the storm of the century in the blink of an eye? Before

I know it, gale-force winds and cold drenching rain turn Harvest Festival into pandemonium and hysteria.

It's just a blur—wind-borne debris, deafening thunder, panicked screams, soaked fairgoers scrambling in all directions. I'm running too, wildly, bounced around by the surging crowd more than moving under my own power. And in the middle of all of it, Ava's voice, from the base of the Tilt-A-Whirl:

"Mason?"

I rush to her. How could I not? "It's okay! This can't last long!"

The next thing I know, we're shrinking together as a ferocious gust tears loose the sign atop the ride. It spins above our heads, the sheet metal resounding as it buckles in the powerful wind.

Then it drops, slamming into the wet ground just a few feet in front of us. At the teeth-jarring crash, we jump together and hold on for dear life.

We cling to each other, the vibration of the sign's impact still ringing in our ears. We don't move. I'm not sure we even breathe.

That was close, I think. And when I dare to open my eyes, Ava's heart-shaped face is barely an inch away.

And what do I say in this turbocharged moment,

when the two of us have just almost been killed?

"Hi."

She doesn't pull away in disgust. In fact—I think she's getting closer . . .

Lightning forks across the sky as our lips touch.

The morning after the disastrous opening night of Harvest Festival, our town is barely recognizable. Scattered tree limbs cover everybody's yards, and houses suffer broken windows, ruined shutters, and missing shingles. The metal roof of the Texaco station has been pulled back like the lid of a sardine tin. Pasco Electric Company crews dot the streets, repairing downed wires. My neighborhood didn't get power back until this morning.

Rufus thinks our branch-scattered front lawn is for his entertainment alone. The big sheepdog is all over the property, leaping and climbing, rolling around the fallen leaves and broken twigs. It looks like half the yard is attached to his shaggy coat. I seriously doubt the Shop-Vac is going to survive its next dog grooming.

Then again, I'm not exactly thinking straight. My mind is whirling faster than the windstorm that caused all this damage. The images flash through my brain like a movie played at triple speed—the blinding explosion of the blown transformer; the panicked crowd rushing the exits; the Tilt-A-Whirl sign slamming into the ground; and Ava, her eyes huge in the chaos of the moment—

"Mason, get your head out of the clouds!" My father stands, struggling with an armload of fallen branches. "I'm ready for the twine!"

"Sorry, Dad." I loop the rope several times around the twigs and knot it, forming a tight bundle.

Dad tosses it on top of the pile at the curb.

Ava! It was all such a blur that I'm not even sure I can trust my own memory of what happened under the Tilt-A-Whirl last night. What if the falling sign landed on my head and I dreamed the whole thing? No, it was real. It had to be. Nothing so huge, so *important* could be a figment of my imagination. I kissed her and she kissed me back.

I can feel a smile forming on my face, and I quickly chase it away. I kind of suspected before, but you never know till you know.

Now I know. She likes me.

Our big moment only lasted a few seconds. When the fire department arrived and evacuated the fairgrounds, we were caught up in the stampede of people running for safety. The parking lot was a madhouse of worried parents looking to rescue their kids, blaring horns and phone flashlights deafening and blinding everyone. Before we had a second to talk about anything, Mr. Petrakis dragged his daughter off to their SUV, and home. I haven't been able to reach her since. My calls won't go through, and my texts are all marked *not sent*. The local cell towers were damaged in the storm, so phone service has been spotty. That might even be a good thing. What would I say to her that wouldn't sound goofy?

I'm actually kind of grateful for the confusion of last night and the fact that the whole town is upside down this morning. It gives me the smokescreen I need to keep from admitting to Ty that I broke the non-Ava treaty. Oh, man, I didn't just break it. I smashed it, blasted it down to its component atoms. How could I do such a thing? I understood the rules; I helped make them up!

My one consolation is that Ty doesn't know anything about this. Not that Ava and I can keep it a secret forever. But maybe there's a way to hold off on telling Ty until it doesn't upset him quite so much anymore. I can't imagine exactly how or when that would be, but surely there's some situation where Ty will be in such a good mood that he won't care. Like what if we give him the news on the day his mom gets elected president, his dad wins the lottery, and geologists strike oil in the Ehrlich backyard?

Nope. Not good enough.

Well, how about the day that Ty gets a girlfriend?

Oh, sure. Ty's prized possession is a paperweight containing volcanic ash from the eruption of Mount Saint Helens. I'm sure the ladies are lining up.

Or maybe the two of us have been such good friends for so long that Ty will forgive me. It's such a happy thought I can almost make myself believe it—until I imagine a reverse scenario, where it's Ty who broke the treaty.

No, that's not going to work either.

"Mason"—Dad sounds exasperated—"go rescue your dog before he skewers himself like a shish kebab on one of these branches."

I snap out of my reverie in time to see Rufus, poised on a fallen limb like a high-wire artist, his ample belly dangling mere inches above a razor-sharp spike. I race across the front yard, clamp both arms around the sheepdog, and tackle him away from danger. The two of us end up muddy and breathless in the flowerbed.

Rufus hops free, shakes himself, spraying dirt in all directions, and bounds away in search of more trouble.

Spitting soil down the front of my sweatshirt, I sit up and find myself staring at a pair of denim-clad knees. Ty reaches down and hauls me to my feet.

"How's it going?" I'm determined to sound natural in spite of my nervousness. "Did you guys get a lot of damage at your place?"

Ty shrugs. "Couple of broken fence posts. My mom's garden gnome is MIA. Where were you when the storm hit?"

"In my room," I lie. "I thought the roof was going to come off. The wind sounded like a freight train."

"Really?" Ty's tone is flat. "So what you're saying is you weren't at Harvest Festival?"

I gulp. He *knows*. But how can he know? Ava and I were alone at the Tilt-A-Whirl! No one was there. The people were all running for the exits.

My mind races. Ty can't know about the kiss. It's impossible. But maybe—just maybe—somebody caught a glimpse of me in the crowd and mentioned it to Ty.

Ty's eyes narrow. "What's it going to be, man? Were you at the fair or not?"

I'm sweating now, which is turning the earth on my cheeks to mud. "Well, yeah, I *was*—before the bad stuff. But it was boring, so I went home. That's where

I was when the storm hit."

"Yeah," Ty agrees. "You look real bored." He holds out his phone.

The picture on the screen nearly stops my heart. I recognize the Tilt-A-Whirl first, even in the low light. And the two figures standing there, locked in an embrace that's been looping through my brain, triple-speed, ever since—

My voice is papery. "Where did you get that picture?"

"Everybody has it," Ty replies accusingly. "It's on the seventh-grade chat."

"Impossible! The cell service is down!" To prove my point, I pull out my own phone, knowing that the gesture is pointless. Even if every cell tower in the state has been vaporized, there's no denying the image Ty is holding right in front of my face.

When I look at my own screen, my heart sinks. Service has obviously been restored. I have twenty-eight new messages, eleven of them from Ava. "I can explain—"

"We had a *treaty*!" Ty cuts me off. "The Romulans and the Klingons, remember?"

"The sign blew down!" I'm babbling now. "We both could have gotten killed—"

"You can't break treaties!" Ty rages. "The safety of the whole galaxy depends on them! I held up my end of the bargain! And what did you do? *The total opposite of that!*"

"It was the circumstances! The *storm!*"

"It was a non-Ava treaty! What could be simpler than that? You only had to do *one thing!*"

"I—I—I—" There's nothing to be said. I'm a million percent in the wrong, and we both know it. Plus, I tried to lie my way out of it, making everything that much worse. I look him squarely in the eye. "I screwed up. I'm sorry."

Ty's face flames bright red. "I don't care how sorry you are. You and I are not friends. Not now. Not ever."

I stare. *Not friends.* I'm shocked to hear the words, but on another level, I understand I shouldn't be. We've both always known that this could be the only result of a treaty violation. That's why we needed the treaty in the first place. We were both so smitten with Ava that the idea of her with one of us would throw our friendship completely out of balance. If the tables were turned, I'd feel exactly the same way.

This isn't just a disagreement or even a fight. It's a tear in the fabric of the universe.

"I'll make this right," I plead hoarsely. "I promise."

"Nothing can make this right" is his response.

I'm devastated. *Not friends.* For Ty and me, even the idea is ridiculous. Unthinkable! And yet, I can't even argue with him. We practically share a single mind. I understand perfectly how final Ty's pronouncement is. How strange is that—to know someone so well that you can see that your friendship is doomed?

"Hi, Ty!" Dad waves from across the yard. "Come on inside. There's hot chocolate brewing."

"No, thanks, Mr. Rolle. I've got to get home." He adds in a lower voice, "I'm done here."

8

SEVENTEEN YEARS OLD

Question: What's harder than getting your science-fair project into the car?

Answer: Getting it out again.

My foot presses down on the forward-folded driver's seat as I try to wrestle the bulky project out of the back of my nine-year-old Volkswagen Beetle. The corrugated cardboard of the display bends against the doorframe as I inch it along, grunting and sweating.

"Need help, Mason?"

I know that voice. Even without turning around, I'd know it out of a thousand voices. Ava.

In an awkward motion that's designed to seem natural but probably looks like a muscle spasm, I throw an arm in front of the title plate of my display box—actually three boxes joined together. No way can I let her see that this project is called Possibilities of Time Travel. It's exactly the same project that she, Ty, and I were working on back in seventh grade.

That project—the seventh-grade one—was never finished because *it* happened. The *thing*. What would you even call it? There has to be a word for what happened between Ty and me. A falling-out? Not strong enough. A fight? Keep going. Less than murder, but not by much.

Possibilities of Time Travel—the original version—was the first casualty. People can't work together if they won't even look in each other's direction. The astronomy club went next. Poor Ms. Alexander—now Mrs. Nekomis. It almost broke her heart. And the greatest friendship in history, obviously.

It wasn't Ava's fault, but she was caught in the middle of it. She had no way of knowing there was a treaty that bore her name, or that she was helping me violate it. But when Ty and I went from best friends to mortal enemies overnight—over *that* night—she was smart enough to put two and two together.

She blamed herself. Worse, whatever connection might have been blossoming between her and me died instantly and was never allowed to be reborn. Ava pulled away from both of us. Dominic, Miggy, and the popular kids were more than happy to welcome her into their crowd.

So how can I let her see that I've completed *that* project from another lifetime, five years after the fact? She'll think I'm pathetic. Worse, she'll think I'm still mooning over what happened behind the Tilt-A-Whirl when we were both twelve. What a loser! Still stuck in seventh grade.

"I'm good, thanks." The effort to keep my arm in front of the title threatens to dislocate at least one shoulder.

She pauses, peering into the car. "Science-fair project?"

"Still the science dweeb," I acknowledge with a forced smile.

She grins. "I remember those days. Good luck." And she moves off, breaking into a run to catch up with some friends. She has lots of those. After she split away from Ty and me, Ava turned into the popular girl she was always meant to be.

Don't get me wrong: It's not like I'm a hermit. I can find kids to hang out with if I want. But the kind of friendship Ty and I had—that was a lightning strike, a one-in-a-million shot. Who could understand a freak of probability better than two champion mathletes?

I slick back my tuft of hair and make another try at getting the giant project out of the Volkswagen. This time it pops free suddenly and I almost go flying. I shut the door with a hip check and begin the long struggle across the parking lot, stepping carefully, since I can't see the pavement over the display carton.

Once in the school, I get a lot of dirty looks trying to maneuver the oversize project through the crowded halls. I have to kick at the stairwell door before someone opens it and lets me squeeze through. Turning sideways, I start up the steps. Kids coming down from the second floor stream around me, some of them jostling the display box.

And then the door to the second-floor hallway opens, and out walks none other than Ty. He's struggling with his own science-fair project, contained in a corrugated cardboard display even bigger than mine.

Figures. It's like the whole universe is configured to remind me of what we lost.

Stepping carefully, because he can't see the floor either, Ty starts down as I continue up. We meet in the middle and grind to a halt with the two projects pressing against each other. There's no way that the bulky displays can pass in the narrow stairway.

"Back up," we chorus in perfect unison. Even after five years of un-friendship, we still speak with one mind and one mouth.

"No, *you* back up." Also in unison.

I sigh, exasperated. "Listen, we're both good at science. This is a math problem, nothing more. If you lift *that* end, and I swing *this* end around here . . ."

I give him credit. He goes with it at first. We both shuffle, shift, and adjust until Ty's project is squashed against the wall and mine is balanced precariously over the banister. There's still not enough room. If this really *is* a math problem, the universe of solutions is the empty set.

"Hey, Spaceman," comes a voice from below. Dominic. "You want to shove off?"

"Some of us have classes to get to," adds his loyal sidekick, Miggy.

Like those guys would ever cry their eyes out over missed school.

Ty and I are jammed dead center in the stairwell, trying to shuffle-step past each other without crushing Ty's display or dropping mine down to the basement.

Bad enough to have a worst enemy without having to be plastered up against the guy, practically cheek to cheek.

That's when I notice the title plastered along the top of Ty's display box: *Time Travel: The Possibilities*.

"Wait a minute!" I practically choke. "What's that supposed to be?"

"My project!" Ty replies belligerently.

"No, it isn't! It's *my* project!" With great effort, I turn my project on its perch on the banister, revealing where it says: *Possibilities of Time Travel*.

Ty's eyes bulge. "You stole my idea!"

"You stole *my* idea!" My eyes focus on a silver-clad action figure of an astronaut on the left side of Ty's display. "Is that my Buck Rogers?"

"No, it's *my* Buck Rogers," Ty retorts. "You gave it to me for my eleventh birthday."

"That's a collectible! You never should have

taken it out of the box!"

"It's none of your business what I do with *my* stuff!"

At this point, we're yelling to be heard over the ruckus around us. There's a full-fledged traffic jam in the stairwell as students trying to get up or down become trapped behind the two unmoving projects.

Tempers flare and angry voices ring out.

"What's going on up there?"

"Get out of the way! I'm late for class!"

"It's Spaceman," Dominic chimes in. "He and his spacey friend are having a supernova about something."

The late bell rings, adding an air of urgency to the general confusion. Now the crowd is pushing from both upstairs and downstairs, with Ty and me trapped in the middle. The noise level rises by at least twenty decibels.

Part of Ty's display board tears in the middle and is smashed flat against the wall. The Buck Rogers action figure drops out and bounces down the stairs, disappearing under dozens of feet.

"Look what you did!" Ty rages. "This is your fault!"

"My fault?" I echo. "You're the one who wouldn't get out of the way!"

"What's going on here?" Mrs. Nekomis bursts onto

the scene from the first-floor hall and gawks in dismay at the chaos in the stairwell.

"It's Mason and Ty!" Miggy tattles. "They're blocking the steps!"

"Everybody off the stairs!"

Mrs. Nekomis starts up, moving students bodily out of her path.

Face flaming red, Ty drops his ruined project and shoves me into the banister. There's a crunch as the corrugated cardboard display is crushed between my weight and the wrought-iron rail. Model pieces and papers sail out of the open box and all the way down to the basement. Horrified, I drop to the stair in a desperate attempt to keep my hard work from disappearing forever. It's too late. The box is broken, the papers still fluttering.

"Cut it out, you two!" Mrs. Nekomis demands shrilly. "You used to be—"

I don't want to hear it. I see red. All I can think of is my project is wrecked and someone has to pay. In a blind fury, I leap to my feet, swinging what's left of the display box at Ty.

It strikes a glancing blow on Ty's shoulder. The impact tears my model of the International Space Station free of the project. It hits Mrs. Nekomis full in the face, shattering into a million pieces. It's not a heavy blow, but it's enough to startle her and throw off her balance.

With a cry of shock, she tumbles backward down the stairs and comes to rest near the bottom step.

The stairwell, which resounded with shouts not two seconds before, is suddenly as silent as a tomb.

Mrs. Nekomis stares up at me in shock and anger. A narrow trickle of blood makes its way along a face that's a thundercloud.

9

SEVENTEEN YEARS OLD

Dear Mrs. Nekomis,
How are you? . . .

I slam the pen down and tear up the paper in disgust. What kind of question is that? I know exactly how she is—all beat up and bruised from her trip down the stairs, thanks to me.

According to my mother, the good old-fashioned handwritten letter is a lost art form. Good riddance to it is my opinion. It would be so much easier to send a text or an email to say the same thing, but Mom insists that a "real letter" will mean more. So here I am.

Dear Mrs. Nekomis,
Let me explain what happened on the stairs that day.
Funny thing—it was actually Ty's fault . . .

I rip that one up too. She doesn't need to hear my excuses, even if they're one thousand percent true.

Dear Mrs. Nekomis,
I'm so, so, so, so sorry . . .

I examine my work critically. Okay, maybe cut out a few of the *so*s. But that's the message I'm shooting for. I feel absolutely horrible about what happened. And not just because I got suspended. Because I hurt the best teacher I've ever had.

Suspension is the kind of thing that happens to the Dominics and Miggys of the world—kids who are always getting in trouble. Not to me, with my towering grade point average and my applications to colleges like Stanford and MIT. I can only hope all this is straightened out before it lands on my permanent record—potentially screwing up everything I've been working toward all these years. My stomach tightens at the thought of it.

I'm anxious about that, but mostly, I feel awful for Mrs. Nekomis.

I experience a stab of anger at the thought of Ty. *He* isn't suspended. Talk about unfair! Ty isn't being blamed for any of this, when he was fifty percent of the standoff that led to Mrs. Nekomis's accident. A week of detentions—that's all he got. A slap on the wrist! True, *I* was the one who swung Possibilities of Time Travel, launching my space station model into the teacher's face. But he forced me to do it by ruining my project. How come he's not sitting at home while senior year passes him by?

Another problem with being suspended from school: Moping around the house all day makes me miss Rufus so badly that it's almost a physical ache.

It's weird. I don't even miss *Dad* that much—although my father isn't dead, just divorced. Still, it's been more than a year since Rufus tangled with that Roto-Rooter truck and came out second best. You'd think I'd be used to it by now. Yet I still half expect to see the sheepdog come bounding down the hall, his furry face wet from drinking out of the toilet.

Now that I'm suspended, the long hours at home only serve to point out Rufus's absence more than ever. Without him, the house seems empty—no barking, no clicking of canine toenails on tile, no grinding of the garbage disposal, which Rufus had figured out how to turn on with a nudge of his huge snout. First he'd hit the switch; then he'd start whining because the noise scared him. The big guy had style. He would lie under the living room coffee table, and every time he sneezed—which was a lot—he would smash his head first on the underside of the glass top and then on the floor. *Achoo—bang—thump!* I'd give a lot to hear that sound one more time, or to feel the jolt of ice-cold nose when Rufus used to greet me after a day at school.

But there's no point focusing on that. Rufus is dead and my status at school is on life support. *Suspended until further notice*—those were the principal's exact words. The further notice is scheduled to come half an hour from now at a special disciplinary meeting with Dr. Lalonde. Mom is taking an extended lunch so she can meet me at the school. That's when we'll find out how long the suspension will last—how long I'll be sentenced to puttering around this house, chasing the ghost of Rufus while I eat myself up with guilt over my poor injured teacher.

I push the unfinished letter aside, grab my jacket, and head out to the Volkswagen. No point in putting it off any longer. The car's starter whirs feebly a few times, and for a moment I toy with the awful thought that I'm going to be late to my own sentencing. I whack the dashboard in exactly the right spot—above the center heating vent. The engine catches in a blue cloud of burnt oil. I'm on my way.

Turning into the parking lot, I'm actually glad to see the school. Nothing like taking something away to make you appreciate it. I make a promise to myself then and there: I'll keep my head down for the rest of senior year. My total focus will be on studying and making this up to Mrs. Nekomis. Like, I can go over to her house and offer to rake leaves, because maybe her arms hurt too much for her to do it herself. I'll definitely come up with something.

At the office, the security guard scans my driver's license and prints me a visitor's badge even though I show the guy my student ID.

Mom is already there, her forehead creased with worry.

"It's going to be okay," I tell her. "It was just an accident."

Nervously, she reaches out and tries to smooth down my tuft. "Let's hope Dr. Lalonde sees it that way."

Dr. Lalonde is a tall bald man with a fringe of gray hair and a long straight nose. He offers us each a glass of water, and I take him up on it. Suddenly, my mouth has gone Sahara dry.

Mom leaves her glass untouched on the principal's desk. "All right, give it to us straight. How bad is this?"

Dr. Lalonde's expression becomes pale and grave. "I'm afraid it's as bad as it gets, Mrs. Rolle. I'm sure that you know the district has adopted a zero-tolerance policy regarding any behavior resulting in injury to a teacher."

I swallow hard. "I'm so sorry about that. I'd never hurt Mrs. Nekomis—she's been my favorite teacher since middle school! She must know I didn't do it on purpose!"

The principal's brow furrows, but he forges on. "I realize you meant no harm. Yet harm was caused nonetheless. As much as I'd like to intervene, it's out of my hands. This comes straight from the district office."

My mother slumps in her chair. "How long is Mason

going to be suspended for?"

Dr. Lalonde sighs heavily. "You misunderstand me. Mason isn't suspended at all. He's expelled."

I snap to attention. "Expelled? Like kicked out? Forever?"

The principal nods unhappily. "Believe me, Mason. I tried to intervene on your behalf. I explained to the school board exactly what happened. Even Mrs. Nekomis spoke up for you. But the new guidelines are very specific. If any harm comes to a faculty member at the hands of a student, that student is gone. No exceptions."

It's as if the whole world tilts and I'm suddenly struggling to stay in my chair, like I'm on a twisting carnival ride. Expelled? Me? I'm a straight-A student, a science star, a teacher's pet, a goody-goody! I'm so good I sometimes make *myself* sick!

"But Mickey Zelinsky threw an M-80 in the furnace, and she didn't get expelled!" I protest. "The whole school could have gone up! That's all the teachers, not just one!"

"I understand this must be a terrible shock," Dr. Lalonde says sympathetically. "And I regret it. Honestly."

"But where's Mason going to go to school?" Mom

almost wails. "How's he going to graduate?"

"You'll be able to make a special application to the surrounding districts," the principal assures her. "And, of course, there's always the private-school option."

"That's all there is to it?" I'm amazed. "You get booted out of one school, and you just pick another?"

"No," the principal admits. "I won't lie to you. With an expulsion on your record because of violence toward a teacher, it will be difficult to find a new school. Perhaps somewhere that specializes in behavior problems—"

My mother leaps to her feet. "Mason doesn't have behavior problems!"

Dr. Lalonde doesn't even have the courage to meet her eyes. "Maybe it won't come to that," he almost mumbles.

I stand up. "Come on, Mom. I think we're finished here."

I walk out of the office without waiting to be dismissed. Why should I? Lalonde isn't my principal anymore. I can still hear Mom pleading my case, almost in tears. Isn't there anything that can be done? How can an honor-roll student be thrown under the bus like this?

Eventually, the sound of her voice is drowned out by the roaring in my ears. Nobody gets expelled. Detentions, sure, by the week—by the month. Disciplinary actions up the wazoo. Suspensions. Never *expulsion*. Not for an M-80 in the furnace, or vandalizing the boys' locker room, or even driving a pickup truck through the plate-glass window of the cafeteria. And not for Ty, who's every bit as guilty as I am.

It would be funny if it wasn't so life-changingly awful. I'll never get accepted into another school—not a decent one, anyway. And what does that leave? A school for "behavior problems," Dr. Lalonde suggested. A place where every kid is like Dominic the Dominator, only twenty times worse. A guy like me—who lets Dominic and Miggy get under my skin with a nickname like Spaceman—wouldn't last ten minutes.

And that's the best-case scenario. What if I can't find a new school in time to graduate this spring? That means no college next year. And what college would have me anyway, with an expulsion on my record? I think of my applications sitting in the admissions offices of some of the most elite universities. The trips across the country to visit campuses and take the tours. A student with my grades and my accomplishments should have his pick of anywhere he wants to go. Yeah, right.

I'm doomed.

All at once, I need out of this place. I burst through the heavy doors that open into the parking lot, but I don't get more than a few steps before the weight of what's happening causes my legs to fold under me and I sink to the pavement. The sheer unfairness of it presses down on me, and I can't get up again. What's the point of being a good kid—of trying hard and doing homework and following rules and being respectful to teachers—if one lousy accident can ruin your life for keeps?

I'm not sure how long I've been sitting there when someone grabs my arm and hauls me to my feet. Mom. Her face is tear-streaked, but her eyes are dry, and her expression is sheer determination.

"I know how upset you are, but don't panic. I'll see if your father can come over tonight so we can discuss this. I have to get back to work."

"You're leaving me?" The one thing I haven't anticipated is having to bear this alone, even for just a few hours. The mere fact that Mom considers this serious enough to include Dad proves that we're in Code Red.

"They need me at the office," she explains. "I'll call your father from there. Maybe we can get a lawyer and fight this."

"You heard Lalonde!" I protest. "He said it's zero tolerance."

She wraps her arms around me, and just for a second, I'm tempted to collapse into them and cry the way I did when I was little. "Try to relax," she advises in a tone that sounds about as unrelaxed as it's possible to be. "We'll deal with this as a family tonight." She rushes to her car and drives away.

I'm rooted to the spot long after she's disappeared from view. The only thing that starts me walking toward the Volkswagen is what I can see out of the corner of my eye—the security guard watching through the front window. For all I know, I'm about to be forcibly removed from school property. That's what I get for thirteen years of straight As. Well, I won't give them the satisfaction!

The car starts on the first try—at least I can spare myself the humiliation of being asked to leave. As I screech out of the parking lot, my mind is still in the narrow stairwell that fateful morning—Ty and me, our matching science-fair projects at a standoff on the steps, neither of us willing to give way as mobs of kids build up behind us both.

Even now, knowing what the consequences are, I can't imagine what I could have done differently to avoid this terrible fate. Moved aside on the stairs, probably. But even then the two bulky projects wouldn't have been able to pass in such a confined space. I would have had to back all the way down—or Ty all the way up. And how could we with crowds of students above and below?

I make a left turn onto the main road, the Volkswagen spewing blue smoke as it accelerates up to speed. I have to admit that it didn't help that the other person involved in the science project impasse on the stairs was Ty. There's just been so much bad blood between us over the years.

All that was put in motion half a decade ago, when two best friends became two mortal enemies. That was the moment that *really* set up this disaster. The old Mason and Ty wouldn't have gotten into such a scrap over our science projects. The old Mason and Ty wouldn't have done two separate projects in the first place. We would have been partners, like we'd always been in the past.

If I'm honest with myself—brutally honest—the seeds of getting expelled were sown when I was twelve years old, on the night of Harvest Festival when the big storm blew through. When I violated the treaty by kissing Ava Petrakis by the wreckage of the Tilt-A-Whirl sign.

That night—that wild night! I barely remember that kiss, and I still don't know who took that picture of us that ended up on the seventh-grade chat. But it cost me the greatest friendship I'll ever have. And now, five years later, it's ruining my life. Here I am, racking my brain over what I could have done differently three days ago, when the moment that really could have made a difference took place at that Harvest Festival.

If I had it to do over again, I'd change everything! I'd honor the treaty, I wouldn't kiss anybody, and there'd be no picture on the seventh-grade chat for Ty to see!

By now, I'm slamming my fists against the steering wheel, blinded by frustration and rage. Which probably explains why I don't see the furniture van turning out in front of me until it's too late.

I slam on the brakes, kicking my heel into the pedal so hard I'm afraid my foot will blast clear through the floor. The rear of the VW swings around as the car goes into a spin. My last thought is: *I'm not going to be able to stop in time.*

I hear screeching tires and smell burning rubber in the split second before the crushing jolt of impact.

Everything goes dark.

TWELVE YEARS OLD
SEPTEMBER 12

I lurch awake, choking on thick liquid trickling down my throat.

With a shudder of horror, I remember the accident. *Blood!*

But no—the taste is salty. Almost foamy—

I sit up with a start. Now that liquid is splashing down on my head. I look around, disoriented. How come I'm not sitting in the middle of the road? Where's the car? The street? The daylight?

I'm in a darkened room, wrapped in heavy fabric—a sleeping bag. And the liquid is being poured on me by a shadowy figure in a ski mask.

"Hey—cut it out!" My voice is higher-pitched than it's supposed to be.

A plastic bottle hits the floor beside me, splashing the sleeping bag.

There's a click, and the room is flooded with light, momentarily blinding me. When I'm finally able to blink myself back into focus, I recognize the science lab. Only—it's the *middle school* science lab! What am I doing *there*? I haven't been in the middle school in years!

Several other sleeping bags dot the floor, with middle school kids in them. This is some kind of sleepover! And there are *two* masked invaders, laughing diabolically and running for the exit. At last, their handiwork begins to appear amid the group—hands placed in bowls of water, magic-marker mustaches drawn on upper lips. Words like *NERD*, *DWEEB*, and *LOSER* decorate foreheads. Random pieces of lab equipment have been knocked everywhere. A cracked beaker oozes bubbling chemicals onto the tiles. I spot the plastic bottle beside me, still spewing liquid. Hydrogen peroxide.

That's when I see Mrs. Nekomis at the light switch, trying in vain to intercept the intruders as they blast out the door. I'm overcome with regret at the sight of her—until I suddenly realize that she's totally unmarked by her tumble down the stairs. What happened to the scrapes and bruises? Three days ago, the science teacher looked like she lost a fight with a Bengal tiger! Now she's totally fine! Nobody heals that fast! She even seems younger. And her hair is longer—

"Mrs. Nekomis?" My voice is still higher, wrong.

She stares at me. "Who's Mrs. Nekomis?"

"*You* are!"

Her attention shifts from the two disappearing intruders to me. "Mason, are you all right? You're spitting foam!"

"They poured hydrogen peroxide in my mouth!" I complain in that voice—almost a little-kid voice.

The teacher drags me over to the sink so I can rinse my mouth out with water. When I catch my reflection in the mirrored wall, it practically stops my heart.

It's not me!

No, it is *me*—Mason Rolle. But it's not me *now*.

It's me from middle school!

I gawk at myself—the twelve-year-old face; the bristly stick-up hair, the way I used to wear it before

I figured out how to grow it long and slick it down. Across my brow has been written the word *SPACE-MAN.*

I wheel and take in the sight of the middle schoolers crawling out of their sleeping bags. That kid—the one with *DWEEB* scrawled across his forehead—that's *Ty*! Not Ty now, twelve-year-old Ty! And there's Clarisse—still wearing her braces! I examine the faces, trying to add five years to each one. I know them all—at least I *knew* them all! This is the astronomy club Ty and I formed in seventh grade—the lab sleepover Mrs. Nekomis chaperoned so we could watch the Orionid meteor shower. Only she wasn't Mrs. Nekomis back then, she was—

"Ms. Alexander?" I breathe.

The teacher leans forward in concern. "Are you sure you're all right? You're not foaming anymore, but you're very pale."

Well, why wouldn't I be pale? I have every reason to be! Just a few minutes ago, I was in a car accident, and now I'm *here*. And where is here? The middle school! But the real question is: *When* is here?

The calendar on the wall provides all the information I need.

That's five years ago! What am I doing here?

I rack my brain, but the only explanation that makes sense is terrifying in the extreme. I'm not actually in this lab half a decade in the past. I'm in the wreckage of my car, hallucinating and dying. And all this is my short life flashing before my eyes. Which means I could wink out and be gone forever any second now.

Even though I know the moment isn't real, I cling to it. It's the last piece of my life I'm ever going to get to experience.

Ty—seventh-grade version—puts a hand on my shoulder. "Dude, are you okay? You don't look so hot."

In spite of everything, I feel a surge of happiness. If this is my final moment, at least I'm getting one from before Ty and I had that terrible fight. We're friends again. I'm grateful I get to experience that one last time.

"I'm good, man," I assure him, "now that you're here."

Ty gives me the nose-wrinkle frown. "What are you talking about? I was always here."

Clarisse puts her two cents in. "You guys are weird."

Ms. Alexander checks her watch. "Maybe we should

call your parents, Mason, and have them pick you up. I think you've had enough of this sleepover."

"I don't think they can get here in time," I muse.

"In time for what?" Ty demands.

How can you tell your best friend that you could be dead at any second?

Ms. Alexander is already dialing her phone. "That settles it. I'm calling."

"You're a great teacher, Ms. Alexander," I inform her emotionally. "I'd never push you down the stairs on purpose."

Clarisse is wide-eyed. "What was in that hydrogen peroxide?"

"Ask Dominic and Miggy," I reply. "They're the ones who pranked us."

"Hold your horses," Ms. Alexander warns. "I agree it was a rotten thing to do, but we have no proof of who it was."

"I do," I assure her.

"How can you be so certain?" the teacher demands. "None of us saw their faces."

I shrug. "They brag about it tomorrow."

Throughout all this, I'm fully expecting to blink out of existence at any moment. But here's the thing: I don't—not in the science lab, and not when Mom pulls around the school's circular drive to pick me up twenty minutes later.

There's somewhat less gray in her hair, but it's definitely my mother of five years before. "Hi, Mom!" I greet her heartily.

"What are you so perky about?"

She sounds groggy, and I note on the dashboard clock that it's 1:14 a.m. She was probably sleeping. "Sorry to drag you out so late."

She softens. "Ms. Alexander says there was an incident, and you're acting a little—mixed up."

"I'm fine, Mom." *Incident*—not a bad description of the car wreck that kills you. But I don't think I'm dead yet. Maybe I'm *not* at the accident site, hallucinating all this as my life drains away. Which begs the question: What am I doing in the middle of my own life from five years ago?

"Then what's the story, Mason? Have you lost your interest in meteor showers?"

"I just—couldn't sleep." She doesn't buy it, and I know why. I sleep like a rock, and always have. "I got lonely. I missed you guys."

"Oh, *please*. You sleep at Ty's as often as at home, and I never have to come pick you up. What's with you tonight?"

I wish I knew.

As we pull into the driveway, I notice the basketball hoop is still over the garage. If this whole thing is a hallucination, it's super accurate. That hoop got knocked down by a falling branch during the storm on the opening night of Harvest Festival.

Correction: It *will be* knocked down, but it hasn't happened yet. That's obvious, since Ty and I are still friends. Also, the Orionid meteor shower sleepover happened *before* Ava moved to Pasco. So whatever I'm doing in this weird moment, I'm in the pre-Ava era.

As I lug my rolled-up sleeping bag into the house, I can't help but snicker at the gray porcelain umbrella stand by the front door. "I can't believe we still have this! I thought you got rid of it years ago!"

"Mason, you're scaring me!" my mother exclaims. "It was here at seven o'clock when you left to go to the school!"

I laugh harder. "It looks like an elephant's leg! See? The bottom is the foot and that beading is the toenails!"

She's annoyed. "Well, if you always thought our things were so awful—"

She says more, but I don't hear a word of it. The approaching clicking noise freezes me like a statue where I stand. The sleeping bag drops from my nerveless fingers. I'd know that sound anywhere. It's—it's—

"Rufus . . ." I mouth the name, but nothing comes out.

The sheepdog rounds the corner from the back hall, where his bed is. I race to greet him, and the two of us meet in a joyful embrace that knocks me over. A giant sloppy tongue kisses my face all over.

"Rufus—you're alive!"

That does it for Mom. "Bad dog, Rufus! Leave Mason alone! Can't you see he's not feeling well?"

"I'm feeling great, Mom!" I blubber, grabbing fistfuls of shaggy fur. "Rufus is here!"

"Rufus is always here!" she counters. "Like a bad smell!"

"You don't understand!" I stammer. "The Roto-Rooter truck—" Of all the terrible things that have happened, even the car accident was worth it to share one more hug with my dog.

"I'm taking your temperature." Mom starts for the bathroom to get a thermometer.

"What's going on?"

I stare. It's *Dad*, padding barefoot down the stairs, blinking away sleep!

"You *live* here!" I blurt.

Dad's eyes widen. "Of course I live here! Where do you expect me to live?"

Serena is right behind him—nine-year-old Serena. "Mason?" It comes out *May-shon*. The palate expander.

"Hi, guys!" I greet them jovially. The last time I saw Serena, she was an obnoxious high school freshman, coming off a growth spurt directly into an awkward phase. "You're cute again!" I exclaim.

"Mom, Mason's scaring me!"

My mother returns, separates me bodily from Rufus, and sticks the thermometer in my mouth. "No talking," she orders. "I want to get a good reading."

I don't give her an argument. Maybe the thermometer will explain what I can't—why am I trapped in this moment from the past, five years before that furniture van pulled out in front of the Volkswagen?

TWELVE YEARS OLD
SEPTEMBER 12

My temperature turns out to be normal.

Maybe so, but it's just about the only normal thing about me.

Mom decides that all I need is a good night's sleep. I lie in bed in the Battlestar Galactica pajamas I'll outgrow in eighth grade, staring at the room that's mine and yet not mine. The model of the solar system that Rufus tore down—correction: *will* tear down. That model is in mint condition now—right down to the extra blob of glue on Neptune from when Ty sneezed as we were putting it together. Man, we laughed that night!

I'm glad to see some of my old posters: the earth as viewed from space, the periodic table in Elven runes, a labeled diagram of a velociraptor skeleton; Darth Vader in a ballet tutu—I don't even remember what eventually happens to that one. The corkboard is there too—displaying my collection of pins and badges—so this must be before the roof leaked and the metal backings got rusted out.

Why am I in this place? Why am I in this *time*? Up until now, I was pretty much convinced that all this was a dream caused by my car accident. But it's been going on for hours now. If I'm going to die, why hasn't it happened already? And if I'm not, why haven't I woken up?

What else could this be? Reality? That would mean my teenage years, my high school career, my parents' divorce, losing Rufus, the rift with Ty, getting expelled—all that was a hallucination, and I've been twelve the whole time? Impossible! You can dream about being older, but not five full years of life experience!

Am I losing my mind? Maybe. The shock of getting

expelled could do that to a guy. But then I'd be a high school senior who thinks he's twelve. I stare at my too-small hands. I wouldn't actually *be* twelve.

Well, I *am*! I'm in my twelve-year-old room, wearing my twelve-year-old pajamas, in the same house as my still-married parents and my dog who isn't dead yet. And in the science lab at school, I just left a bunch of kids the same age as me—and they're all twelve.

And Mrs. Nekomis is Ms. Alexander again.

Could this be time travel? It's been favorite subject number one for Ty and me ever since we were old enough to understand the concept of time and space. It was the science-fair project we were working on with Ava when we had the big meltdown in seventh grade, and the project we'd both choose independently as high school seniors. Could I be time traveling and not even know it? If so, it isn't anything like Ty and I always pictured it. Not like the movies, where a modern person goes back to the Revolutionary War. And not like the real science, where astronauts have experienced a few less seconds on their journeys than actually ticked off back on Earth. Never once did we consider that you'd go back to your life exactly as it was at that time.

On the other hand, this isn't *exactly* the past. I didn't

get sent home from the Orionid meteor shower sleepover the first time around. I'm not doing and saying the same things as I did back then. And for sure, I'm not *feeling* the same things. As if to prove my point, Mom opens my door a crack and peeks inside, and I pretend to be asleep—none of which could have happened originally, because I slept at school. And as I remember it, I really did sleep, instead of tossing and turning all night, wondering what's happening to me.

Eventually, the stresses of the day—which began five years in the future—catch up to me, and I fall into a deep slumber.

Dr. Sewicki makes a few notes on the chart and smiles. "Well, Mason, you're fit as a fiddle. If I was as healthy as you, I'd run a marathon every day."

I hop down from the exam table and nearly twist an ankle. I'm six inches shorter than my seventeen-year-old former self, and I thought I'd be a lot closer to the floor. "So I can go?" I ask, hugging the flimsy gown around me.

"In a minute," the doctor replies. "First I want to talk about this unusual behavior your mom's so worried about."

I hesitate. Maybe I should tell Dr. Sewicki the whole

story. A trained doctor might be able to explain what's happening. On the other hand, the doctor would probably decide that the craziest part of all this is actually me. Better to keep quiet and see how things play out.

"I woke up at a school sleepover, and I was kind of confused for a while. That's it."

The doctor is unconvinced. "Twelve is a funny age. Puberty and all that. I'm sure you've noticed certain changes in your body."

I nod. Changed and changed back. Dr. Sewicki doesn't know the half of it. Going from seventeen to twelve in one day is some serious change.

"Are you sure there's nothing you'd like to tell me?" the doctor probes.

Well, I drove my car into a furniture van yesterday, but I'm not sure that counts since it won't happen for another five years. Aloud, I say, "I'm okay."

Dr. Sewicki seems satisfied with that. Later, as I get dressed, I overhear him in the hallway telling Mom, "Kids can be peculiar at this age. Maybe he failed a test or a girl looked at him funny. We'll probably never know."

Or maybe he's been parachuted back from the future.

We walk to the Beetle, which was my mother's car before I inherited it. It's already getting old and quirky, even now. When she twists the key in the ignition, the starter whirs but doesn't catch. She tries again. Same result.

Automatically, I reach over and give the dashboard a whack in the usual spot above the center vent. The motor roars to life with the next twist of the key.

Mom stares at me. "How did you know to do that?"

"Beginner's luck," I tell her. It's easier than explaining that, five years from now, it's the only way to get the darn thing started. If I say that, she'll march me straight back into Dr. Sewicki's office.

We start for home, and I find myself stepping on an imaginary accelerator on the floor of the car. To go from a high school senior with a driver's license to a twelve-year-old who depends on parents to get me everywhere is a pretty big comedown. Also, was Mom always such a wimpy driver? Seriously—at the four-way stop, she won't turn until there's enough space to fit a freight train between her and the next vehicle. And the speed—or lack of it. Just because the limit is forty doesn't mean you should go eighteen to be on the safe side. No wonder the Volkswagen is falling apart. It's probably dying of embarrassment. I spend the ride with my teeth firmly planted in my tongue to keep me from saying something.

When we finally pull into the driveway at home, Ty is waiting on the porch swing. At first, I'm taken aback to see him there. I have to remind myself that we're not seventeen-year-old enemies. This is normal for us. I let myself enjoy the feeling, since I doubt whatever's happening will last much longer.

"I brought your homework," Ty informs me.

Something I haven't considered yet: Do I actually have to do this? Not that it would be very hard for a seventeen-year-old to do seventh-grade homework.

But that's beside the point. Is this my life now? Am I twelve-year-old Mason Rolle from now on, destined to relive my teenage years—if I ever really lived them the first time around? Do I have to have my tonsils out again, and sit through that BTS concert because Serena loves them? Or is this some kind of time blip, and I'm about to wake up seventeen again exactly the way I woke up twelve? And of course, option three: Am I dying or even already dead? Not the happiest possibility, but I definitely don't want to bother doing homework in that case!

Aloud, I say, "Thanks, I think," and accept the folder.

Mom opens the door, and I make it about three feet into the house before Rufus bowls me over and slobbers all over the homework. I'm still overjoyed to have the dog back, but I'm remembering how gross the big guy could be. Rufus was—*is*—a drool factory.

Without being invited, Ty follows me to my room. It feels a little pushy at first—but obviously, it's another example of the way things used to be. I would do the same thing at Ty's place. It's all returning in a rush of memory.

Once we're alone in the shadow of the solar system model, Ty asks, "You're not sick, right?"

"No." Dead, possibly, but not sick. "The doctor says I'm fine."

"How did you know it was Dominic and Miggy who pranked us in the lab?" Ty persists.

I shrug. "It's always them. When's the last time anybody else did something that rotten?"

Ty is unconvinced. "That doesn't explain everything, man. Last night, you said they were going to brag about it today. And that's exactly what they did. How did you know *that*?"

"How did you *not*?" I counter. "Those two big mouths could never resist a chance to brag. They can't think far enough ahead to realize they're getting themselves in trouble."

"You've got that right. Ms. Alexander slammed them

both with detention for the next three days. That's about how long it'll take me to wash the permanent marker off my face." He looks me over critically. "You should do some scrubbing too. I can still see Space-man on your forehead."

It sinks in that last night might have been the first time I was ever called Spaceman, a nickname I carry clear into senior year—assuming all that was real. I'm almost reaching the point where I can't assume any-thing anymore.

"Well, you didn't miss much," Ty goes on. "The meteor showers were kind of *meh*. Too cloudy and not much of a light show."

I actually remember that sleepover as being a lot of fun, in spite of Dominic and Miggy's antics. As I recall it, the Orionids were pretty nice. Then the astronomy club went back inside the lab and made s'mores. It was really cool until Ty gummed up one of the Bunsen burners with melted marshmallow and Ms. Alexan-der got bent out of shape about it. He was always the clumsier of the two of us. Mrs. Ehrlich used to tell my mom she'd take me in a trade, because I never fell over my own feet. Anyway, that's another piece of evidence that I'm not reliving my life exactly the way it hap-pened the first time around.

Ty opens his backpack and pulls out his books and iPad. He expects that we're going to do homework together, like we've been doing since first grade. It's the last thing I have any interest in. I'm a) hallucinating, b) crazy, c) expelled, d) in a car wreck, e) lost in time, or f) actually dead. And Ty expects me to focus on math problems?

Fine, math homework it is. It's not like there's anything else I can do to straighten out my life at the moment. Besides, how hard can it be for a guy in Advanced Placement Calculus to knock off seventh-grade math?

If Farmer Garcia builds an A-frame barn that's 17 feet high at its tallest point . . .

Ty peers up from his own paper. "What's taking so long?"

I glare at him. He's almost halfway through the page, and I'm struggling with question one. "Don't rush me."

"You just have to calculate the volume of the barn to figure out how many hay bales fit inside—"

"Listen, man, I haven't done this in five years, so give me a break, will you?" I explode. He regards me in bewilderment, so I quickly add, "I'm *kidding*. I just—I—uh—"

Utterly defeated, I push my paper in his direction. He reaches over and scribbles a quick calculation.

"Oh, right," I say. "Got it."

And later, while doing social studies, Ty is staring blankly at his iPad when I lean in with his stylus and call up the right Google search.

"Thanks."

It goes on like that for almost an hour—the two of us doing not just our own homework, but each other's as well. By the time we're finished, I remember that this used to happen every day—and that homework was a lot easier and a lot less boring when we did it together.

When Ty tries to segue from schoolwork to video games, I come very close to kicking him out. My whole world is unraveling. How can I waste my time playing games with a twelve-year-old?

But I'll never be able to explain that to Ty, who thinks I'm a twelve-year-old too. It's coming back to me that homework followed by video games is a routine we've had since forever. Pretty soon, we're flat on our bellies in front of the Xbox, battling a dragon outside King Arthur's court.

The controller feels just a little too big—or maybe my hands are just smaller than I'm used to. But as I'm learning—first from Rufus, then from Ty—the old ways come back fast.

I haven't played Continuum since that terrible day when Ty and I stopped being friends. It was our favorite game by far, and no small part of our obsession with time travel. I think I gave it up to punish myself because I was the one who broke the treaty.

I share a high five with Ty as his character hoists the Grail on the screen.

"This game's awesome," Ty declares, flushed with victory.

"Yeah! Only"—I sit up suddenly—"how come all the time-travel things are always hundreds or thousands of years ago? You know how, in games and movies, everyone goes back to ancient Greece or the Civil War? How come nobody ever time travels, you know, five years into the past?"

Ty thinks it over. "Well, you could, but it wouldn't make much of a story. The whole fun is traveling back to a totally different world. But nothing much changes in just five years."

My mind whirls. Mom and Dad, still together; Rufus, still alive; Ty and me, still friends. It's pretty clear that a whole lot can change in five years.

"Besides, it's complicated," Ty goes on. "If you go

back only five years, what if you meet a younger version of yourself? But you never met your *older* self when you were that age, so you could be messing up the whole timeline. It might not even be possible."

It brings on a rush of memories. The two of us used to go back and forth for hours on end with the what-ifs of time travel. But I don't have the energy for it today.

What's different? Today it's not a what-if anymore.

I'm living it.

TWELVE YEARS OLD
SEPTEMBER 16

Walking Rufus is like trying to control a comet at the end of a lasso. A leash means nothing to him. He drags you along faster than you can possibly walk, and he can never quite figure out why he's choking.

It's a great workout, though—something between a two-step and a jog. Not too fast—I always have just enough breath to call, "Aw, come on, Rufus! Slow down!" Which Rufus never does. Possibly, he can't hear me over the sound of his own wheezing.

Cleaning up after Rufus is a major operation. After the deed is done, I feel like I'm walking around with a plastic bag full of cannonballs. The nearest trash can is never close enough.

Afterward, in the dog park, I let go of the leash to give the sheepdog some freedom. Rufus romps around, drinking out of puddles, chasing candy wrappers, and snapping at butterflies. Suddenly, the big guy stiffens like a pointer, fixing a laser gaze in the direction of the road. A square white van emblazoned with the Roto-Rooter logo is putt-putting along the street. The dog's hind legs tense, ready to spring his large body forward.

"No-o-o!!" I dash forward just as Rufus pushes off and starts for the road. *"Heel!"* Now, what's the point of that? Rufus never had a minute's obedience training and never obeys for a minute. He doesn't come when you call him; he has that *who's gonna make me* look on his face at all times.

But Rufus dies in an accident with a Roto-Rooter truck! The panicky thought flashes through my head as I run. That's not supposed to be for another four years! But a lot of things aren't happening the way they happened before. What if the timeline has changed? What if it's today?

I leave the ground in a flying leap of desperation. My reaching hands grasp hold of the end of the leash a split second before I thud painfully to the dirt of the dog park. Wildly, I yank back just as Rufus lunges for the cube van.

My *oof* and Rufus's yelp come at exactly the same time. The white truck continues down the road. Lying stunned on the grass, I reel in the leash like an angler landing a giant swordfish. Rufus fights the pull every inch of the way—until the truck is out of sight. Then the big guy trots over and licks my badly scraped cheek. It's Rufus's most endearing quality. He can go from total warfare to clueless and sweet in the blink of an eye.

I'm panting and breathless, not to mention bleeding. "You smelly hairball, you want to get yourself killed?" Okay, this wasn't the moment I know is coming one day—the one when a Roto-Rooter truck just like this puts an end to Rufus. But that moment will arrive eventually if Rufus can't get over this weird obsession. *"Bad dog!"*

Rufus may not be the brightest canine in the animal

kingdom. But if there are two words he understands perfectly, those words are *bad dog*, because he hears them twenty times a day. First his ears droop. Then his tail stops wagging. Finally, his whole hairy body slumps to the ground, and he lies there, a picture of shame.

I stand up and dust myself off. "It's okay." I cave. I always cave where Rufus is concerned. "I didn't mean it. You're a good dog."

Knowing he's forgiven is a big deal to Rufus. He jumps up, slobbering all over my bleeding hand, which only makes the sting twice as painful.

"But no more Roto-Rooter trucks. You hear me?"

Obviously, Rufus can't understand that. What dog could?

I make a mental note to google dog-training tips. Rufus is not going to die at the hands of the Roto-Rooter corporation if I have anything to say about it.

TWELVE YEARS OLD

SEPTEMBER 19

Every morning, I wake up fully expecting to be seventeen again—although I almost wonder why I'd want that. Seventeen-year-old me is expelled from school. I've been in a major car accident. I could be injured, or even dead. I've made an archenemy out of my closest friend. The more time I spend in my twelve-year-old life, the clearer it becomes that throwing away the friendship with Ty was the dumbest thing I ever did.

Anyway, I don't have to worry about that. At the sound of my alarm, I blink the sleep out of my eyes, and my gaze focuses on the hundreds of pins stuck to the cork wall beside my bed. I remember being really proud of the collection at age twelve, but from a seventeen-year-old perspective, it has to be the goofiest, most pointless thing anybody ever collected. And I don't even keep it in a box somewhere, to be sorted through once in a blue moon. I have to display it on my wall so it's the first thing anybody sees when they enter the room. I get that I'm not exactly an icon of coolness at seventeen either, but at least I had the brains to delete the picture of my cork wall from my Instagram story.

I should probably give my twelve-year-old self a break. Five years is a long time, a lot of life experience. Seventeen is a man, almost old enough to vote. High school seniors don't bother with kid things like pin collections or action figures—or at least, only with the classic ones that are kind of timeless. You know, original 1960s Star Trek characters, still in the package, like Mr. Spock. I scan the shelves anxiously, before remembering that I won't buy Spock until eighth grade—still a year away.

I think back—*ahead?*—to the silver-clad Buck Rogers figure Ty used in his high school science-fair project that day. Out of the package! Ruined! I should give Ty a piece of my mind about that—only how can I chew the guy out for something that he won't even do for another five years? He'd think I'm nuts—and he'd probably be right. Of all the explanations why I might be taking this excursion through my past, that's the one that makes the most sense. But am I a seventeen-year-old who thinks he's twelve? Or a deluded twelve-year-old with false memories of five teenage years that never happened?

I'm kind of caught between anger at Ty for the enemies we're about to become and gratitude for the amazing friends that we still are right now. If there's a silver lining to the black cloud of being banished to my seventh-grade self, it has to be him. Seventeen-year-old me forgot how it felt to have someone in your life you can be totally yourself with, knowing you'll be accepted and understood no matter what. When I thought back to Ty as a lost friend, I didn't remember the half of it. How comfortable we used to be, how we never argued or even disagreed—except when we were debating time travel or distant galaxies or superpowers in one of our marathon conversations that lasted late into the night. How one of us could burst out laughing into his chocolate milk, and the other would instantly understand the joke based on the sound of the gurgling and choking.

When the door slams downstairs, I know it's Ty collecting me so we can walk to school together—because we *always* walk to school together. So that makes—I check my phone—exactly eight hours and forty-two minutes since our final text from last night. And at least eight hours of that apart time was spent asleep.

I throw on some clothes, give my teeth a quick brush, and splash some water on my stick-up hair—knowing I'll already feel it rising again as it dries on the walk to school. Then I run downstairs and freeze, momentarily unable to process the fact that this twelve-year-old is Ty. Only a look in the hallway mirror reminds me that I'm twelve too.

"Dude," Ty greets me.

"Dude," I acknowledge.

I grab a cereal bar and select one from the peanut-free box for Ty. He rips off the wrapper and takes a bite without even checking the ingredients. Mom stocks our pantry with a selection of Ty-friendly snacks, just like the Ehrlichs always lay in a supply of plain potato chips because I can't stand the texture of Ruffles.

"I finished *Planetoid* last night," Ty is raving as we

start for school. "Dr. Cirrus comes back from the graviton mines of the Horsehead Nebula. Bet you fifty bucks he takes over when Administrator Volkov retires."

"You're on," I reply. I know for a fact that Dr. Cirrus gets killed off halfway through season two. Then again, if I'm still twelve by the time that happens, I'll have bigger problems than fifty dollars can solve.

I hold out my fist, but before we can seal the deal with our secret handshake, Ty suddenly drops out of sight. The next thing I know, he's rolling on the grass next to the green garbage bag he tripped over.

"What the—?"

"Sorry." I haul him upright again. "Dad's too lazy to put pants on over his boxers to take out the garbage, so he tries to throw it from the front porch to the curb."

Ty sizes up the breadth of the front lawn. "He needs a good pitching coach."

"It really bugs my mom," I add, stuffing a ketchup-smeared paper plate back in through a hole in the plastic. "It's one of the reasons they got divorced—" I catch myself too late and clam up.

Ty stares at me for a moment and then bursts out laughing. "Yeah, right! My mom says your folks are the most rock-solid couple in the neighborhood."

I carry the garbage bag to the curb, hiding my face so Ty won't see the flush in my cheeks. I have to stop talking about the future. That kind of thing can only get me in trouble.

Walking to school every day takes a little getting used to. Walking anywhere is kind of frustrating when you've had a driver's license for more than a year. The only thing worse is begging my parents for rides when the weather's bad, or when I want to go anywhere more than half a mile away. I don't remember it bugging me so much the *first* time I was twelve, but now it feels dehumanizing, almost like Mom and Dad get their jollies out of watching me grovel. For sure, it's something I won't miss when I get back to my regular life.

If I get back to my regular life.

If my regular life even existed.

"Heads up!"

I'm barely three steps into the schoolyard when Ty's warning makes me jump. There's no time to react before an enormous force plows into me from behind. My backpack is ripped from my body, nearly removing both arms at the shoulders, and I'm shoved to the ground.

"Morning, Spaceman." Dominic stands over me, shaking the backpack like it's a beautifully wrapped birthday present and he's trying to guess what's inside. "What've you got here? Moon rocks?"

"Give that back!" Ty lunges for the bag, but Dominic throws it effortlessly to Miggy.

"Only one way to find out," Miggy concludes, undoing the zipper. He upends the bag, dumping the contents onto the grass. He peers into the pile of books, papers, and gym clothes. "Now, let's see what we've got . . ." He rifles around and comes up with a T-shirt with a portrait of the scientist Stephen Hawking. He squints at the name. "Who's Hawkeye?"

"Isn't he one of the Avengers?" Dominic suggests.

Miggy examines the photograph. "Nah—wrong guy."

I scramble up. "That's Hawking, you—!" I make a run to recover the shirt, but just as I get there, Miggy bunches it in his fist and lobs it to Dominic.

"Come on, guys," Ty pleads. "Give it back."

"Okay, fine." Dominic offers the shirt to me. But just as I reach for it, he yanks it away and holds it high over his head. "On second thought, I'm not done with it yet. I like Hawk-Man!"

"Hawkeye," Miggy corrects.

"Hawk*ing*!" Ty and I chorus.

The picture of Dominic twirling the T-shirt like a lasso triggers something in my brain. I *remember* this! Dominic and Miggy tossed the shirt back and forth while Ty and I chased after it like a couple of clumsy puppies. It went on for so long that pretty soon, half the school was gathered around us, cheering on one side or the other. A few kids were even taking bets on the outcome. Eventually, I got so upset and exhausted that I dropped to my knees and threw up in front of everybody. It was one of the most humiliating experiences of my life.

Well, not this time!

I make a bull run at Dominic, but when the big jerk throws the shirt back to Miggy, I don't pull up and follow it. Dominic's eyes widen in shock as I speed up, lower my shoulder, and slam it into the center of the bigger boy's chest.

The impact rattles all 206 of my bones. It hurts so much that, just for a moment, I toy with the idea that I might not live long enough to make it to seventeen again. I see stars, but then I see something else that makes it all worthwhile—the sight of Dominic Holyoke, the Dominator, knocked flat on his back on the ground.

"Pancake!" Miggy breathes in awe. "Serious line-backer stuff!"

As Ty looks on, terrified, I stomp over and snatch the Hawking shirt from Miggy's fingers.

The Dominator doesn't stay flat for very long. He jumps to his feet and towers over me. I don't shrink away. I can't quite explain it, even to myself. I may be in my twelve-year-old body, but my mind is seventeen. Although Dominic is bigger and stronger, he's still a seventh grader. I'm not backing down to one of those.

Dominic seems surprised that I'm standing up to him. "You watch your back, Spaceman." He storms away, making sure to jostle me as he goes.

Miggy rushes off after him.

Ty is beside himself. "Dude, why did you do that?"

I stick the Hawking shirt back into the bag and set about restoring the rest of my things. "I can't let him push me around forever."

"Sure you can!" Ty exclaims. "Now he's going to kill you! And he's going to kill *me* for being friends with you! Then he's going to come back and kill us both again just to make sure we're dead!"

I honestly wish I could assure him that his fears are unfounded, but I just can't. I didn't knock Dominic down the first time today happened, so we're in uncharted territory. There's no way to predict how the big jerk is going to react to being laid out. Ty might be right. There could very well be a gigantic butt kicking in our future. But if Dominic was going to fight back, why didn't he do it right away, when the attack was fresh in his mind?

TWELVE YEARS OLD
SEPTEMBER 19

The glare Dominic shoots me when I step into Ms. Alexander's homeroom would melt titanium. I get a dirty look from Miggy too, but a more complicated one—maybe mixed with a little respect?

"Hey, Mason"—Clarisse approaches, her voice hushed—"everybody's saying you knocked Dominic unconscious on the playground!"

Ty jumps forward. "It never happened! It's a lie!"

"He wasn't unconscious," I add. "He just went down."

"Well, I say it's about time somebody stood up to those knuckleheads," Clarisse tells me.

"Shhh!" Ty hisses at her, with a nervous glance in the direction of Dominic and Miggy.

The teacher breezes in and we take our seats at the front-row table, with Clarisse opposite us.

"Thanks for that," I whisper to her. Something I've been noticing in the past few days—Clarisse tries really hard to be friends with us, and the way we treat her in return isn't that great. This isn't something I remembered before arriving back in seventh grade to see it firsthand. But it's kind of disturbing to think that Ty and I—for all our complaining about how the popular kids treat *us*—might be a little bit guilty of exactly the same thing.

Ms. Alexander tosses her purse onto her desk. She looks around suspiciously. "All right, let's hear it. What happened?"

It starts slowly, but a rising babble fills the class. I'm not sure exactly who says it, but somehow the statement "Mason decked Dominic in the schoolyard!"

rises out of the din.

Ms. Alexander waits for the cacophony to die down and launches into a long lecture about spreading gossip. "This happens all the time," she says sternly. "The rumors travel from mouth to mouth, and they become a little wilder and more colorful the further they spread. And by the end of it, everybody is completely convinced of something that never happened and nobody with any sense should have believed."

I'm actually insulted. I didn't set out to pancake Dominic, but I resent the fact that my favorite teacher doesn't think I could do it. I mean, I wouldn't bet on me versus Dominic straight up in a cage fight. But is my seventh-grade reputation so wimpy and weak that no reasonable person could accept that I knocked down the school bully one time?

At that moment, the PA system bursts to life. "Good morning, students. This is Coach Gallo. The sign-up sheets are on the bulletin board outside the gym for anybody who wants to play football this season. Tryouts start this afternoon at three thirty sharp. Hope to see you there."

Dominic and Miggy are high-fiving and fist-bumping at their table, just in case any of us have forgotten who the big sports stars are.

Ms. Alexander sighs. "I was hoping for some volunteers to help decorate our hall after school. But I guess this lets out Dominic and Miggy. Is anybody else planning to sign up for football today?"

Austin Stonehart and Rolando Driscoll raise their hands. And before I have a chance to think about it, my hand is up there too.

Ty gawks at me like my head has been replaced by a giant cabbage. "Dude!" he hisses. "What are you doing?"

"All right, Austin, Rolando, and"—the teacher frowns when she reaches me—"Mason? Are you sure about this?"

I nod, although I'm not even a little bit sure. Why would I want to play football? It's not like I've ever been good at any sport before—and I include my teenage years right up to seventeen, which technically haven't happened yet. But when I think about how Ms. Alexander never considered the possibility that I could have knocked Dominic down, it just bothers me. I've already seen that everything in my life doesn't have to go exactly the way it went the first time around. Which means I can make a few tweaks. Like this one.

"Yeah," I gulp. "I'm sure."

"Not only that, but he's going to be great at it!" Clarisse adds with feeling.

Ty kicks her under the table and glares at me. He probably sees the cake-eating grins on the faces of Dominic and Miggy, who are thinking about what they're going to do to me when they get me on the football field.

"It's okay, man," I whisper. "I got this."

When the bell rings and I'm on my way to first period, Dominic and Miggy come up on either side of me.

"Got to hand it to you, Spaceman," Miggy says, shaking his head. "Here we were, trying to figure out how to stomp you into baby powder without getting in trouble, and you come up with the perfect way to make it legal."

"Prepare to be a real spaceman," Dominic advises darkly. "First tackling drill, you're going to the moon."

"No, he's not!" Clarisse tells him. "Mason's going to wipe up the field with you guys!"

Dominic and Miggy find that so hilarious that they cackle all the way to first period.

The person who isn't laughing is Ty. All day, every

time he looks at me, I see a completely different emotion: anger, disbelief, confusion, even pity. At lunch, he gives me his extra taco, and I know for a fact that Ty loves tacos more than he loves his own mother.

"Will you cut it out?" I snap at him. "It's cafeteria food, not my last meal."

He regards me with sad eyes worthy of Rufus.

"Listen," I try to explain, "we've been in the Pasco schools for a long time. And everything we do is always the same kind of stuff. Science fair, astronomy club, Academic Olympics."

"What's wrong with that?" he challenges.

"Nothing. But what respect do we ever get for it? Insults on our foreheads and a mouthful of hydrogen peroxide. What kind of life is that?"

"The live kind," he replies readily. "Which is more than you're going to have when the Dominator gets through with you at tryouts."

"Maybe," I admit. "I'm probably going to get stomped. But what if I've got kind of a knack for it? You heard Miggy when I hit Dominic this morning. He called it 'serious linebacker stuff.' A linebacker is a football player, right?"

Clarisse approaches our table, tray in hand, but Ty tries to scowl her away.

"Have a seat, Clarisse," I say pointedly, and she slips into the bench beside Ty.

"Listen, man," he goes on as if she wasn't even there, "I know we always do everything together, but this time you're on your own. This isn't like Halo, where if you get killed, you respawn. Once a walnut gets cracked, you can't put it back together again. Sorry, Mason. I'm out."

"I wasn't expecting you to do it with me," I say honestly. "It's just something I have to try."

"Well, I think it's great," Clarisse puts in. "I bet you'll get a home run. No, wait—football is touchdowns, right?"

Ty shakes his head at me. "Are you the same kid I've been best friends with, like, forever?"

I honestly don't have an answer for that. Probably something like yes and no.

At three thirty, when I present myself at the field house, Coach Gallo doesn't recognize me. Why would he? I've never played on any team, and in PE class, I make it my business to be as unnoticeable as possible. Apparently, I've succeeded beyond my wildest dreams.

"Do I know you, kid?" he asks, frowning. "How long have you been at this school?"

"I'm a linebacker," I tell him. "I'm really good at— backing lines."

He looks me up and down. "We'll see about that."

I'm half expecting to be given a uniform and pads and be told to go tackle Dominic again—which is probably a lot harder when he knows you're coming. But that's not what happens. Conditioning is everything, Coach explains. So we put on shorts and sneakers and run around the track—twelve times.

On lap one, I'm surprised to see Ty among the handful of spectators on the bleachers.

"Thanks for coming to support me," I call up to him.

"It's not support," he shoots back. "Someone needs to be here to call your dad when it's time to pick up your dead body."

I laugh appreciatively. I'm already a quarter lap behind the lead runners, and they're only half a lap in. But I'm confident I can make the team. This is middle school. Everybody makes the team.

"Pick up the pace, new kid!" Coach Gallo hollers.

I thought I *was* picking up the pace.

I won't try to sugarcoat it. I don't mind running, but twelve laps is cruel and unusual punishment. I'm only on lap three when Dominic and Miggy overtake me from behind. Dominic makes sure to kick my heel out from under me, and I make a five-point landing on knees, elbows, and nose.

"Foul! Where's the flag, ref?" comes a high-pitched voice from the bleachers. It's Clarisse, who's settled herself in the stands next to Ty. "That's two minutes in the penalty box!" She's obviously not a sports fan, so this must be her version of loyalty. It means a lot to a guy lying flat on his face on a track.

Coach Gallo misses Dominic's cheap shot. He hears Clarisse yelling and notices the whole team stepping over me like I'm a human hurdle. Bleeding from all five contact points, I pick myself up off the track, ready to slink to the field house and give up my spot on the team.

But then Miggy's mocking voice reaches me: "Check it out! Spaceman crash-landed!"

That stiffens my spine and starts my legs pumping again. I don't remember how I was at twelve, but seventeen-year-old Mason Rolle has a much higher pain threshold and a much greater storehouse of cussedness. I don't care if my life's supply of blood drains out right here on this track. I am not giving those oafs the satisfaction of making me quit.

Miggy and a couple of the other faster guys get done

when I'm still on lap seven. Pretty soon, everyone else is finished, and I'm the center of attention, all alone on the track.

Coach Gallo steps out in front of me. "Okay, kid. That's enough."

When I slow to a walk, it's all I can do to stay upright. It might be that the movement of my legs was the only thing keeping me from collapsing.

He goes on. "Football requires a lot of toughness and stamina. Maybe it's not for you."

I want to protest, but I don't have the breath. So I shake my head vigorously.

"Look at yourself," he adds. "You're way behind, you're sucking air, you're bleeding all over my track. Do both of us a favor and go home."

I start running again—and this time it feels a little easier than before. Coach shrugs and leads the others in some throwing and catching drills. I ignore them. Nine laps. Ten. Then eleven.

"Come on, Mason!" Clarisse shrieks from the stands. Ty puts his hands over his ears.

As I come around into the final straightaway of lap twelve, the rest of the team is still throwing and catching, but I can somehow tell that every eye is on me. Dropped and bobbled balls skitter across the turf.

Everybody wants to see if I'm going to make it.

I'm totally gassed. My chest is on fire. Every muscle I own is screaming at me to stop. When I stagger across the finish line, I get a very sarcastic ovation, mixed with a lot of raspberries.

"Dial it back, you guys!" Coach Gallo orders. "You think your effort today was any better than his?"

I hear this through the roaring in my ears. The others jog off to the locker room, but I just stand there, bent double, heaving.

"You alive, new kid?" Coach calls to me.

I can't muster the air for a yes, so I wave.

He nods as if a major decision has been made. "See you tomorrow."

TWELVE YEARS OLD
SEPTEMBER 25

make the football team, not that this is a big surprise, since there are no cuts. I'm officially a Pasco Panther—number zero, which might be an assessment of my value to the squad. I don't have a position yet, unless you count punching bag, but I checked, and that's not a real football thing.

I'm the worst player by far—the weakest, the slowest, with the worst hands and no natural ability. Yet for some reason, I get the feeling that Coach Gallo kind of likes having me around. I'm the look-at guy. Every time a player gripes about anything at practice, Coach says, "Look at Rolle—he's ten times more exhausted than you, and he's not complaining!" Or, "Look at Rolle—he just got clobbered and he's right back on his feet!" Or, "Look at Rolle—he's bleeding way more than you, and he doesn't need a break!"

To be honest, I wish the coach would keep quiet about what an iron man he thinks I am, because the other players are starting to get pretty sick of hearing about it.

"Look at Spaceman, he never complains," the Dominator mimics savagely.

"His head got torn clean off, but he doesn't need a time-out," Miggy adds.

They get their revenge on me during tackling drill. Every time Dominic hits me, it's the equivalent of being run over by a freight train. I know I knocked him down that one morning, but he really must have been off-balance back then. Blocking Dominic is like blocking a brick wall—a spring-loaded one that falls over on you the second you bounce off. But it isn't just the Dominator. Miggy takes me down pretty hard too. And none of the other players show much mercy to look-at guy. I want to explain that it isn't my fault

Coach keeps holding me up as an example. The problem is I've usually got the wind knocked out of me.

So the punishment continues.

The only sympathy I get comes from Ty, who watches from the bleachers almost every day. He doesn't understand why I'm doing this, but I have to give him credit. He's got my back a million percent. Even worse than the torture of watching me get killed is the fact that Clarisse sometimes joins him. Those two have a love-hate relationship, minus the love. It irritates him when she cheers "Defense!" when I'm on offense, or "Crush him, Mason! Show him who's boss!" As for me, I'm not a fan of anyone who calls attention to who the boss *isn't*—and who's crushing who. And that's pretty obvious when I'm the guy who's always on the bottom of the pile.

We finish each workout with our round-robin blocking competition. That's when my teammates send me to the locker room with a little extra pain. This time I catch the very worst of it. Dominic lines me up and plants his shoulder in my sternum. If I concentrate, the sound of that hit still reverberates in my ears.

I lie there, staring at the clouds, while the others head for the field house, exchanging high fives. I'm surprised when a hand is extended into my field of vision. It grabs me by the wrist and hauls me to my feet. I find myself standing toe to toe with Miggy.

I'm instantly on the alert. What's this about? Is he planning to finish the job his partner in crime started?

He regards me critically. "You're okay, Spaceman."

I have absolutely no idea what to make of that. Is it a medical report—like to see if Dominic is off the hook for murder?

I almost ask. But at that moment, Ty approaches, so Miggy turns his back on us and jogs off after the team.

"Clarisse says you're going too easy on these guys," Ty informs me with a disgusted look on his face.

"Give the girl a break," I retort. "She's the only fan I've got."

"You don't need fans; you need ambulance attendants."

"I'm pretty sure I'll survive long enough to make it to high school." I have firsthand info on that one.

Ty waits while I change out of my uniform, and the two of us head for home. It's a rare thing to have a buddy who sticks by you even when he's against what you're doing, I reflect with a lump in my throat.

We're about to step off school property when I spot my father's car parked at the curb.

Dad waves out the window. "Get in, guys. I'll run you home."

It's only a two-minute ride, but I'm grateful for it, because every bone in my body aches. We drop Ty off first and then pull into our own driveway.

Dad grins as I limp into the house. "Never thought I'd be picking *my* son up from football practice. Your Nobel Prize ceremony, maybe . . ."

"I'm expanding my horizons," I explain.

"Good idea. I'm proud of you. It's kind of unexpected, that's all. When I think of a linebacker, I picture your sister, not you."

"She's tough," I agree. In the future, high school freshman Serena is emerging as the queen bee of her class. But I'd forgotten that was already well underway in the palate-expander days of fourth grade.

I reach down and pick up the front page of the newspaper, which is leaning semifolded against our famous elephant-leg umbrella stand. "Quick—let's put the paper back in order before Mom gets home."

"Yeah, eventually," he says vaguely, stepping out of his loafers.

"Dad," I remind him, "Mom freaks when the paper is all over the place. You know she's always complaining about . . ." My voice trails off. Suddenly, I can't remember if my mother's complaints have already happened, or if they start at some point between now and the divorce.

"I'll do it," he promises, "as soon as I'm finished making these calls." And he disappears down to his basement office, leaving his shoes in the middle of the hall—another one of Mom's regular gripes. I can't blame her for that one. Serena once broke her wrist falling over a pair of Dad's loafers. Or maybe she will. I'm not sure if it's happened yet.

So I put away the shoes, and I hunt up the various pieces of newspaper Dad left scattered all over the house while drinking his coffee and getting ready for work this morning. I leave the paper on the kitchen counter. It's all there, except the classified ads, which got drooled on by Rufus. Maybe Dad would get around to it, but chances are he wouldn't. He's a pretty flaky guy and my mother is a neat freak.

In the past couple of weeks, the tension between them has been growing. Or maybe I'm just oversensitive because I know where it all ends up.

In divorce court.

TWELVE YEARS OLD
SEPTEMBER 27

've been twelve again for more than two weeks, and I'm starting to worry that I'm stuck here. The longer I spend as my seventh-grade self, the more it feels like my real life.

Oh, sure, I *remember* being older. I haven't forgotten my teenage years, my parents' divorce, the day Rufus got hit by that Roto-Rooter truck. And how could I ever block out that catastrophe in the stairwell that sent Mrs. Nekomis tumbling and got me expelled? Or the car accident that—

That did what? Killed me? Scrambled my brains and made me hallucinate? Knocked me five years back in time?

I don't think I'm dead anymore. Whatever this is, it's been going on way too long to be my final fever dream before I kick the bucket. It doesn't feel like death; it feels like life—*my* life.

I'm even getting used to this smaller, younger body. It makes sense—it's me, after all, not some random stranger. But I no longer hop out of bed and nearly twist an ankle because my legs should be longer. I've stopped feeling my cheek to see if I need a shave, only to find it smooth. I don't reach for the driver's door of the Volkswagen anymore. I'm controlling my natural impulse to get behind the wheel and pull away. Twelve-year-olds don't do that.

I guess what I mean is I'm rolling with it. Partly because what choice do I have? If I tell anybody what's really going on, they'll lock me in a padded room. But partly because it's not a bad deal. I've got both parents. I've got my best friend. I've got my dog. I'm not expelled. I'm doing okay here. And in the meantime, I'll just keep my eyes open for a clue to what's going on and how I can set things back to normal.

I'm even getting a little bit cocky about my new old life. Of all the kids at Pasco Middle School, I'm the only one working on round two. Face it, if you're given a second shot at something, you're a lot more likely to get it right. I'm not saying I'm suddenly popular—or even borderline acceptable. I get zero percent cred for being on the football team. Dominic and Miggy continue to devote their lives to picking on me. I'm still Spaceman. But I have a kind of confidence too—the confidence of knowing that nothing that happens can possibly catch me off guard.

"We have a new student in our homeroom," Ms. Alexander announces. "Class, this is Ava Petrakis, who comes to us from New York City. Let's all do our best to make her feel welcome."

My neck whips around so fast that I'm amazed my head doesn't snap off and roll across the floor. It's her! Ava! I whiplash in the opposite direction and check the calendar. September twenty-seventh—that was the day Ava came! It's happening again!

Ty leans over to cast me a meaningful look, but this time I don't meet his eyes. Ava—the same silky auburn hair, the same intelligent, lively blue-green eyes and heart-shaped face. She looks a lot younger than she did the last time I saw her in the high school parking lot in senior year, but it's definitely the same girl.

Just when you think you've got seventh grade nailed, along comes life to throw you a curve. It's my own fault. How could I have forgotten something so earth-shaking? Ava showed up on September twenty-seventh last time, and here she is again, right on schedule.

"How many times did you get mugged in New York?" Miggy pipes up.

It's past my lips before I even know what I'm going to say. "I'll bet you just have to put out a vibe that you don't want to be messed with, and nobody messes with you."

Ava regards me in surprise. "I was going to say almost that exact thing." Then, without being prompted by the teacher, she carries her backpack over to our table and sits down next to me. "This seat taken?"

That's when it hits me: The disaster of my seventeen-year-old life—ninety percent of the bad things that happened were set in motion on the night of Harvest Festival, when I broke the treaty with Ty by kissing Ava under the Tilt-A-Whirl. The same Ava who I'm meeting for the first time right now! It's important that I get this relationship off on the wrong foot!

"You have to move!" I blurt.

"Why?" Ty goggles at me. "Nobody sits there!"

"Well, no—not *now*," I babble on. "But remember that kid from last year? The one with the really itchy contagious rash?" I stare at Ty, hoping for that ESP-like best-friend connection to kick in, so he'll realize that I need Ava to get lost pronto.

Doesn't it figure? For the first time ever, the best-friend connection is disconnected. "What rash?"

"Don't pay any attention to Mason and Ty," Clarisse advises Ava. "Sometimes they make sense. Not often. I'm Clarisse."

Ava shakes hands with Clarisse and Ty. But just as she's reaching for me, she stiffens and starts scratching all over. "Oh, no! I think I'm getting a really itchy contagious rash!"

I laugh and she laughs with me.

It's my first official mistake of the Ava Petrakis Story, version 2.0.

"What do you think of Ava?" Ty asks on the way to the science lab.

"Not a fan," I reply briskly.

"Really?" He's astonished. "I think she's awesome. I can't believe she chose to sit at our table out of the whole class. I thought Dominic and Miggy were going to lose it."

I shrug. "She was standing at the front of the room. Ours was the nearest empty seat."

"Yeah, and about that—what's with the hooey about the kid from last year, the one with the itchy rash?"

"Get a sense of humor much?" I defend myself. "I was kidding. Who cares where Ava sits?"

But I do care. I care a ton. An idea is forming in my head, and it's happening so fast that I barely have a chance to think it through. I'm not just reliving a random stretch of seventh grade; I'm reliving the time when I made the greatest mistake of my life. Now that Ava's here, I have a chance to make sure I don't repeat it. I have to fix things so that Ava and I never become friends.

When we get to science, the first thing I do is take the empty stool between Ty and me and move it to the farthest corner of the room. So when Mr. Esposito invites Ava to join one of the other pairs, there's no open seat at our table.

"Pull up over here," Dominic invites.

"Yeah," Miggy adds. "Treat yourself to a free upgrade."

Smiling, Ava walks over to them, picks up their

extra stool, and carries it over to our table. She sets it down between Ty and me. "Hi, guys. Miss me?"

It probably won't work to make up another kid with another itchy rash.

And at lunch, when she breezes over to our seats, makes herself at home, and launches into her entire life story, I try to make a stand while there's still time to save myself.

"Listen, Ava, we get that you're this fancy New Yorker and we're a bunch of hicks here in Pasco, but you don't have to rub it in our faces that your old school had a sushi bar and we're lucky to get mac and cheese once a week!"

Ty is horrified. "Dude! She's not rubbing it in our faces! We're just talking!"

The huge eyes fill with remorse. "Sorry," Ava tells me. "I didn't mean it to come out that way. I know I just moved to Pasco, but I really like it so far."

Doesn't it figure? I'm trying to save my life here, and *I* end up the bad guy.

TWELVE YEARS OLD
SEPTEMBER 30

have a new dog-training strategy with Rufus. Every Saturday morning, I take him down to the Roto-Rooter office. We stand across from the entrance to the parking lot and watch the trucks go out. If he tries to chase one of them, I pull back on his leash and sternly say, *"No!"* If he just watches it go, he gets a doggie treat. If he ignores it completely, he gets two doggie treats.

So far, I'm saving a lot of money on doggie treats. I think Rufus might be starting to get the hang of it, though. He still can't resist going after the trucks. But when I yank on the leash, he barks in perfect unison with my *"No!"* and then looks up at me expectantly, waiting for praise. The security guy is keeping an eye on me out the back window of the building. He's probably wondering why I spend my Saturdays standing across from Roto-Rooter, yelling at my dog. If he reports me to PETA, how am I ever going to explain that I'm doing this to save Rufus?

Speaking of preventing bad things from happening a second time, my efforts to avoid repeating the Ava Mistake aren't going much better than my dog training. She's so self-assured and confident that no matter what I say to her, she doesn't take it personally.

The kid who does take it personally is Ty. "Why do you have to be so mean to her?" he hisses as we walk to school on Tuesday morning. "She's never anything but nice to us."

"I'm *not* being mean to her," I retort, which is a total lie. Every single day, I go out of my way to make her feel unwelcome—which I hate doing, but what choice do I have? How else can I stop this runaway train of fate that's destined to ruin my life when I'm seventeen?

I give her a hard time about sitting with us in class and at lunch. I've even invented a fake sensitivity to lavender, which is the scent of her shampoo. And how does she react to that? She switches to apple-cinnamon. The girl is impossible! She's so *nice* that you can't be nasty to her. It just doesn't work.

"You are *so*," Ty insists. "What is it about her that pushes your buttons? She's the perfect friend for us! She's good at school. She's into all the things we're into. She's cooler than the cool people, because she could totally be one of them, but she wants to hang out with *us*! And she's even interested in time travel. Seriously, if you'd asked either of us what are the odds that the most amazing girl in school would be interested in time travel, we both would have said zero percent."

The one thing Ty's *not* saying is the main cause of all of this: Ty is totally crushing on her. I know this because, the first time around, we *both* were. He's the same twelve-year-old, meeting Ava for the first time. It's me who's older and wiser.

That's the whole problem. I'm being mean to Ava

to keep from losing my best friend. But the way I'm treating her is making Ty so mad at me that I'm in danger of losing my best friend anyway. I'm caught between a rock and a hard place.

"I've got nothing against Ava," I defend myself. "I just don't want to partner with her on a science-fair project. That's a you-and-me thing, like every year. You know the rule: no third wheels. We said no to Clarisse when she wanted to work with us."

Ty makes a face. "You can't compare Ava to Clarisse. That's like comparing Zeus or Poseidon to the god of vegetable soup."

"That's harsh, dude," I tell him disapprovingly. "And anyway, there's no god like that. Not even the Romans have that one, and they've got a god for everything."

"Plus, it's *time travel*," Ty persists. "Our dream topic."

"Nothing is stopping us from doing time travel just the two of us," I remind him.

"You mean steal Ava's idea? Not cool, man."

And he's right. We nerds don't get a lot of respect in the world, but we have an honor code toward each other. You don't wear the same Halloween costume as one of your friends, and where projects are concerned, you never steal someone else's topic. It's an unwritten law.

We're not arguing exactly. But by the time we make it to school and head for homeroom, something's happening that's never happened before in the entire history of our friendship. We can't agree—and neither of us is willing to budge a millimeter.

Ty pauses in the doorway of Ms. Alexander's room. "Listen, if you refuse to work on time travel with Ava and me, that's your problem. But I'm doing it."

I feel my breakfast rising up the back of my throat. I practically choke over the words. "Fine. Clarisse—want to be my partner for the science-fair project?"

There's dead silence in the class. Even Ms. Alexander is staring at us, openmouthed. Most of the kids have known us since elementary school. We're practically considered one person. Never before have Mason Rolle and Tyrus Ehrlich worked on two separate anythings, much less a science-fair project, our claim to fame.

"Seriously?" Miggy pipes up. "Are you telling me Thing One and Thing Two aren't going to be partners?"

"Thing One and Spaceman," Dominic amends.

"That's enough," Ms. Alexander interrupts. "We're all free to work with whoever we choose." But the expression on her face clearly says she can't believe it.

Ava looks uncomfortable. "Am I the problem here? Because I can totally do my own thing."

"Not at all," Ty states positively. "Mason and I are in different groups, no biggie."

He says it like it's just a casual remark, not something about as likely as *Mason and I are taking a space shuttle to another galaxy.*

"I have *tons* of ideas for our project," Clarisse announces, looking like the cat that just ate the canary. "We can do wind turbines. Or golden retrievers. Or build a Foucault pendulum to demonstrate the earth's rotation . . ."

She keeps going—a long list of all the topics for us to choose from. Each one amps up my regret at the decision to work with her. But it's vitally important. Last time around, I worked with Ty and Ava, and we all know what that led to. This proves I have the power to change my destiny.

I catch a stray glance from Ava. The blue-green eyes are filled with hurt, and I feel like a true jerk. There's something else there too—but I can't quite put my finger on it.

TWELVE YEARS OLD
OCTOBER 6

finally have my position on the football team. I'm
bench strength.

Dominic laughs in my face when he hears that.
"Get a clue, Spaceman! Bench strength isn't a real position. It means you sit on the bench because no coach
in his right mind would ever put you in a game!"

I feel kind of torn about that. On the one hand,
Dominic might be right. If you go by how I do in
practice, it's probably not a great idea for me to play in

a real game. I'm the smallest, the weakest, the slowest, and the least athletic. I'm not good at catching the ball, and I have trouble throwing it, too, because my hand's not big enough. I miss most of my tackles, which isn't so bad, because when I do get hold of an opponent, they usually steamroll right over me. And I haven't gotten much of a hit on anybody since I knocked down Dominic before the tryouts even started.

But on the other hand, I've been working really hard at this. I've been to every single practice these past weeks, and I always give it everything I've got. I've devoted more hours to football than I've put into working on the science-fair project with Clarisse. And I *have* improved—Coach himself says so—even if the improved me is still the worst player on the team. For sure, I've got more stamina, and I think my arm muscles might be a little bigger too.

I've *earned* a real position, and I tell the coach that.

He smiles at me. "I like you, Rolle. In all my years of coaching this team, there's never been anybody quite like you. You set a great example."

I know what he means by that. Anybody with as little natural talent as me who goes out for football should have his head examined. So if he ever catches one of the other players dogging it or being lazy, he points to me, bruised and covered in Band-Aids, being an example.

"Example isn't a position either," I point out.

"Fine. You're a cornerback. A backup cornerback."

I've won a lot of quiz bowls and science fairs, but I'm pretty amped up to be this, so I brag about it to everybody who'll listen.

"You're not the backup cornerback," Johnny Camaretti protests. "*I'm* the backup cornerback. And Brett Ramirez backs up *me*."

That's how I become backup to the backup to the backup cornerback of the Pasco Panthers.

By the time I've got my position straightened out, I'm the last one into the locker room to get changed into regular clothes. That's no problem. Ty has stopped coming to practice to wait for me. He and Ava are full steam working on their time-travel project, so he says he's too busy. He doesn't mention anything about being ticked off about my Ava attitude, and I think that's because he likes having her all to himself. Whatever. All I know is it's keeping me away from Ava, and that's what matters.

I take a lot of ribbing from the other players. They chant *"Backup to the backup to the backup to the backup . . ."* while snapping towels at my face. I don't

take it personally, because that's what teammates do—
at least that's what they do in the books I've read and
the movies I've seen. The only real-life teammates
I've had are the mathletes, and they don't trash-talk;
they calculate.

Eventually, they leave me alone to kick into my
shoes. But a minute later, Miggy sticks his head
back into the locker room. "Hey, Spaceman—you
coming?"

"Coming where?" I ask.

"Into town. Friday is fro-yo day. Team tradition."

"I didn't bring any money," I tell him.

"Nobody did," he explains. "It's not about the fro-
yo. It's about who can scrounge the most toppings
before we get kicked out."

That doesn't sound like something I would do. But
the way Miggy describes it, it's a team activity. And as
the backup to the backup to the backup cornerback, I
should be part of it.

Dominic doesn't think so. "What's this loser doing
here?" he sneers when Miggy and I step out of the
field house.

Miggy shrugs. "He's on the team."

Dominic rolls his eyes. "Oh, sure. The backup to
the backup to the—"

All the guys take up the chant: *"Backup to the backup to the backup to the backup . . ."* And before you know it, we're walking down the street, laughing and joking, me included. Dominic doesn't look happy, but he goes with the flow.

Pasco Middle School is only about half a mile from the center of town, so it's an easy walk. I don't think I would have enjoyed it the first time I was twelve, but now I kind of get a kick out of it. These guys think they're so tough, but all they're really doing is punching one another's shoulders and stepping on one another's heels.

At the fro-yo place, the modus operandi is to grab a spoon and try to snarf as many free toppings as possible without the cashier noticing. I get right in there with them, but I don't actually scoop anything. As the one science nerd present, I can only imagine what the microbiome of those sprinkles must be once the Pasco Panthers get through with them. Anyway, it doesn't take long before Dominic gets his hands on the Reddi-wip can, tilts his head back, and empties it into his big mouth. That's when the manager figures out that none of us are topping yogurt; we're just topping toppings. We scram out of there, enjoying our sugar high.

Dominic blows a towering arc of whipped cream

into the road, flaps his lips, and proclaims, "This is boring. There's never anything to do."

Brett, the backup cornerback one backup level ahead of me, has a suggestion. "Let's check out the witch lady."

The witch lady turns out to be the owner of Madame Zeynab's Crystal Ball and Tearoom, a tiny storefront shop on the opposite side of the street. She's really old and wears long, jeweled gowns in faded multicolor prints, the idea being to convince you how supernatural she is. But I guess if you go in there to have your fortune told, or your palm read, or to gaze into her crystal ball, you're already convinced.

The front door is open, and the smell of incense pouring out through the beaded curtain is enough to knock you off the sidewalk.

We stand in a line and make ghostly noises—*ooooooooooooh!* But when the beads suddenly part and her wide, burning black eyes are staring at us, we shut up and take a step back.

Madame looks from face to face as if she's memorizing us. When her terrifying gaze reaches me, it feels like twin holes are being laser-bored into my skull. I wait for the dark eyes to move on, but they stay with me, probing, questioning.

In a gesture that's at once slow and deliberate *and* lightning fast, she reaches out a hand with long painted nails, grabs my wrist, and draws me in through the beaded curtains. And I go, almost powerless to resist, even though her grip is gentle.

Behind me, I hear frantic whispers:

"She's got Spaceman!"

"She's going to eat him!"

"We've got to save him!"

"Forget him! Let's get out of here!"

The words barely register. That's how commanding Madame Zeynab's presence is.

She raises my hand, turns it over, and peers into my palm. Her brow, wrinkled already with age, furrows even more deeply.

"You have—two futures," she tells me.

"No," I reply in a shaky voice. "Just one. I've already been there."

That seems to confuse her, but the intensity of her gaze doesn't waver. "Two futures," she says again. "Two paths."

"Do you believe in—" I promised myself I wouldn't reveal my secret to anybody. But the fortune-teller seems to see something in me that no one else can.

Otherwise, why would she focus on me out of all the Panthers? "Time travel?"

The black eyes grow even wider. "So *that's* the explanation."

"*What's* the explanation?" I exclaim. "You have to explain it to *me*!"

That's when Miggy grabs my arm and hauls me out through the beaded curtain. "Time to go, Spaceman!"

"No!" I protest. "I'm not finished with Madame Zeynab!"

"Never mind her!" Dominic snaps. "I think the fro-yo guy's calling the cops! We've got to get out of here!"

And before I know it, I'm being hustled up the street and we're all on our way home.

I head back right after dinner, my excuse being that I'm walking Rufus. But by the time we get downtown, the tea shop is closed and dark.

I'm devastated. I have to talk to Madame Zeynab! She's the only person with half a chance of explaining what's happening to me. I don't have a clue how she could know that, but she seems to. She didn't pull any of the other players into her shop. I was the only one.

I ring the bell and knock on the glass of the locked

door. "Madame Zeynab?" I call. "It's me—the kid from a couple of hours ago. The one with two futures?"

There's no answer. She's either not there or she doesn't want to see me. And I just can't accept that. I need to talk to her, and I need to talk to her *now*. I pick up a handful of pebbles and throw them against the upstairs window. *"Madame Zeynab!"*

Rufus thinks it's a game. He rushes toward the building to chase the pebbles and is totally freaked out when they bounce off the bricks and fall on him.

"Mason?" comes a familiar voice behind me.

I wheel, but I already know who it is. Ava steps out of the fro-yo shop, a large cone in her hand.

"Oh. Hey," I say in the dismissive tone I always use with Ava. Mostly, I'm hoping she hasn't noticed that I'm yelling the town down for a fortune-teller who isn't even there.

No such luck. She saw everything. "I never pegged you as the kind of guy who'd go see a psychic."

I almost blurt, "She's my aunt!" but catch myself just in time. It would take Ava about fifteen seconds to confirm with her greatest fan—Ty—that Madame Zeynab is most definitely *not* my aunt.

Instead, I go on the offensive. "I suppose New Yorkers are too cool for psychics."

"Just the opposite," Ava replies. "In Greenwich Village alone, there must be fifty little places like this—palms read, tarot cards, crystal ball, soothsayer, séances." She adds, "*You're* the one I thought would be too cool—you know, football player, big man on campus."

"Big man on . . ." I echo before my words peter out. Is she serious? Has this girl even met me? Science dweeb? Cofounder of the astronomy club? Spaceman with the stick-up hair?

That's when it comes to me. Ava loves science, so the dweeb thing isn't a negative with her at all. Plus, she's never known me when I wasn't on the football team with Dominic, Miggy, and the others. She has no clue that I'm the team punching bag, the backup to the backup to the backup. All she sees is that she tried to be friends with me, and I acted like I was too good for her. And instead of hating my guts—which was the plan—it's only made her even more curious about me!

Well, why wouldn't she be? Ava's the kind of person who can walk into a room full of strangers and come out with a dozen new friends. She's nice; she's confident. Dominic and Miggy instantly tried to rope her into their crowd, and they reject everybody.

I glance into the fro-yo shop and confirm that she's

here with Emma and Kennedy from homeroom. But she doesn't just hang out with the popular girls. She and Clarisse are friends too. And Ty says she just joined the recycling club, because she's big on saving the environment. She's all over the place. So when she comes up against my get-lost attitude, it probably makes her want to find out why I'm not instantly drawn to her like everybody else.

Unbelievable! The first time I was twelve, I was in love with her, and she eventually started liking me back. Now I'm treating her badly—and she's started liking me anyway!

I gaze at the multicolored sprinkles on her cone and wonder which of my teammates' grubby germs are on there.

TWELVE YEARS OLD
OCTOBER 10

Clarisse and I finally choose our science-fair topic. We're going to build an infinity mirror to create the optical illusion of LED lights reflected until infinity.

When I say *we* choose the topic, I mean Clarisse chooses it. To be honest, I'm actually not complaining. When you're a super-busy person—like maybe you're trying to figure out why you've ended up five years earlier in time than you're supposed to be—Clarisse is the ultimate partner for a science fair. Not only did she choose the topic; she's doing all the research, building the display, writing up our results, and even recording an audio tour for the judges when they visit our project. All I have to do is show up—or maybe not even that. She probably thinks I'll only get in the way. For all her good qualities, Ty's right about her. She can be world-class annoying. And he doesn't even have the information that I do—which is that five years from now, she's going to be much worse.

I have to admit I feel a little guilty that my total effort on this project amounts to one big nothingburger. But what choice do I have? No matter what suggestion I make, it's guaranteed to be wrong. That's another thing about Clarisse—she's very clear about what's right and what's wrong. And anyway, I justify it all with the fact that, technically, I already did a science-fair project this semester—the twelfth-grade one on time travel that I dropped down the stairs in the altercation with Ty that got me kicked out of school.

Of course, I have no proof of that, so when Ms. Alexander approaches me after homeroom on Tuesday, I'm worried that I'm about to get chewed out for letting Clarisse do all the work.

But the teacher doesn't seem to be angry at all. In fact, I get the impression that she's pretty uncomfortable about something. She keeps glancing over her shoulder to make sure every single kid is out of the room besides me.

"I should probably get going too," I tell her. "First period is starting."

"Not yet." She shuts the door and turns to face me. "There's a new teacher in the music department."

"I'm not in music this semester—"

"His name is Mr. Nekomis," she interrupts. "Remember the night of the Orionid meteor shower? You called me Mrs. Nekomis!"

"Well, I was pretty out of it back then," I manage, inventing rapidly. "Plus, I had a mouthful of hydrogen peroxide, so everything was kind of garbled."

"It wasn't garbled. It was Mrs. Nekomis," she counters. "And when I asked, 'Who's that?' your answer was 'You are.' And weeks later, along comes this new teacher with exactly that name."

Yikes, this is so not ideal. I'm not scared of getting in trouble. In the end, all I have to do is play dumb. But did I just change the future by putting Mr. Nekomis on her radar screen? What if she thinks he's a creepy guy who scouted out one of her students to talk him up to her? They might never get married because of me. This is the kind of time-travel problem that Ty and I used to talk about for hours. What if one of their kids was destined to be president or cure a terrible disease, but now that kid never even gets a chance to be born? All that would be because of me!

It makes me really self-conscious, because lately I've been messing with the future a million different ways—by being mean to Ava, training Rufus to avoid Roto-Rooter trucks, and working on Mom and Dad to try to save their marriage. But who knows what damage I'm doing to the course of history without realizing it?

Very briefly, I toy with the idea of confessing the whole thing to Ms. Alexander. She's a science teacher. Maybe she'll be able to help with my situation. But more likely, she'll get worried about me and call my folks. Or she'll assume I'm being a jerk and pulling her chain, and I'll end up expelled five years earlier than last time.

So I tell her, "Maybe I got woken up in the middle of a dream, and I said something from the dream that sounded like Nekomis. So when you met the new teacher . . ."

"I suppose," she muses. But even her frown is frowning.

"I hear he's a nice guy, though," I offer. "Mr. Nekomis, I mean. The music kids like him."

I have no idea if I've gotten Ms. Alexander and Mr. Nekomis back on track. But for the time being, my parents are still married, so I'm doing what I can to keep them from getting on each other's nerves.

Mostly that involves picking up after my father, since that's the only part of their problems I can have an effect on. I can't do much about the big stuff—like when Dad forgets to pay the mortgage. Basically, Mom doesn't think he's a responsible grown-up. I don't even really disagree with her, but I don't want my parents to split. I love my father, and my seventeen-year-old self remembers how painful the time of the divorce was.

So I put the toilet seat down—much to Rufus's dismay—and hang up all the towels Dad just tosses aside. Outside, I make sure the hose is rolled up after Dad waters the garden. He's okay at yard work, but he's cleaning-challenged, so there are always rakes, shovels, and shears strewn around the property. Mom once got a rake in the face just walking across the grass.

The sad part about the whole thing is that he's a

really great dad—both before the split and after. He always has time for Serena and me, and he's a hundred percent supportive of our interests—no matter how strange they may seem to him. Even after the divorce, he and Mom still get along okay.

I join Mom at the front window one rainy afternoon. "Dad did a good job, right?" As soon as I saw the weather report on my phone, I spent twenty minutes getting everything put away in the garage. One of Mom's pet peeves is "the things we spend our hard-earned money on lying around getting muddy and rusty."

"We need the rain," she comments absently. "We really don't water enough."

"Maybe Dad thinks there's a big storm coming," I put in eagerly. That could earn him points a few weeks from now when half the town blows away during Harvest Festival. "And the newspaper's been nice and neat these days, too, right?" I jam my hands in my pockets so she won't see that I'm covered in newsprint black.

She sighs. "Mason, your job is to go to school and get an education. You don't have to be a cheerleader for your dad."

And when I mention to my father that he and Mom aren't getting into so many arguments over household stuff, he looks at me like that never would have occurred to him in a million years.

20

TWELVE YEARS OLD
OCTOBER 12

Ty and I are still friends—best friends even. But Ava has opened up a big chasm between us.

I don't really blame him for that. He can't understand why I'm not being nicer to Ava, and I definitely can't explain it to him. And now that they're all in on their science-fair project, there's a big chunk of Ty's life that I can't be a part of.

They go to school early every morning to work on the project, which means Ty and I don't walk together anymore. I'm not complaining. That gives me the chance to head into town to see if Madame Zeynab is in her tea shop. She never is. I always get there before she opens. But by the time I run over there after football practice, she's already closed. She may be a good fortune-teller, but I have to question her business model a little. How's she supposed to make money if her shop is never open for customers?

As proud science dweebs, Ty and I don't believe in the supernatural. Everything that happens must have some explanation in physics, chemistry, or mathematics. Even the weirdness that I'm going through now must follow some logical rules of cause and effect. I just don't know what they are yet.

That's why I need Madame Zeynab. She *knows* about me—I saw it in her eyes. But her words didn't make any sense. "Two futures, two paths." What was that about? I have to find out what she meant.

Without Madame Zeynab, there's not much else I can do to try to understand what's happening to me. I did a Google search for *car accident knocked me back in time* without much success. There are plenty of people who *think* they're in the past after a traumatic event, like a car accident or a brick falling on their heads, but they're really in the here and now. One lady who fell out of a tree is convinced she's a handmaiden to Queen Hatshepsut in ancient Egypt. That's not my situation at all. She *isn't* in ancient Egypt, plain and simple. I'm definitely in the past, five years before I started out.

In sheer desperation, I ask Ty if I can see his and Ava's project on time travel. Not that they know any more on the subject than I do—I'm living it and I still know nothing. But they've been researching this twenty-four/seven, and I can't rule out the possibility that some random fact they've dug up might ring a bell with me.

Ty sounds suspicious when I call him up. "I don't think we should let you see our research. You might steal it for your own project."

The mere fact that he could suspect me of that makes me wonder how damaged our friendship is already.

"Why would we steal it?" I reason. "We're building an infinity mirror. At least Clarisse is. I haven't had much to do with it."

He laughs. "Serves you right. That's what happens when you partner with a tyrant."

"So can I see it?"

He hesitates. "Maybe I should ask Ava."

"Who's under the thumb of what tyrant?" I needle him.

"All right," he agrees. "Come on over. Some of the stuff's at Ava's house, but you can check out whatever's here."

Ty's mom greets me at the door. "Prince Mason! Haven't seen you for a while."

And you still haven't, I think, since the real me is five years in the future. But I take her point. Mrs. Ehrlich used to be like my second mother. I mean that literally—back in the day, her name appeared even before Dad's on the list of people who were authorized to pick me up from school. She's used to seeing me at least as often as her own son. The prince thing started with Ty's father. He said I was a prince because I was the only person polite enough to laugh at his corny jokes. I feel a twinge of regret that the need to stay away from Ava is also keeping me not just from my best friend, but also my adopted family.

Ty takes me down to the basement, which is dominated by the cracked terrarium that used to hold the ant farm we created in fourth grade—a rare failure for us.

Ty catches me grinning at it and laughs. "How were

we supposed to know we filled it with the only ants in the insect world that didn't like sugar?"

"And were too lazy to tunnel," I add.

It's a bittersweet reminder of the days when even messing up big-time was fun, because we were doing it together. Man, Mr. Ehrlich was mad when he had to call an exterminator to get the ants out of the basement.

I turn my attention to the time-travel project, which is under construction on the old Ping-Pong table. Another memory—Ty and I never got good enough to play much of a game, so we repurposed the table as our laboratory and makerspace.

I survey their progress. Ty and Ava have the corrugated cardboard display built, but there's no decoration, and none of the material has been mounted yet.

"Ava ordered this wallpaper of spinning clock hands," he explains. "We're going to cover the box with that."

"Nice," I say, not really meaning it. What do I care if he and Ava win the science fair? I'm an infinity-mirror guy—not that I had much choice.

I skim through their research. It's good stuff, but it's nothing new. Printouts from the chronometers aboard the Apollo missions in the sixties and seventies. Einstein's theories and explanations of what happens to time near black holes.

"We're working on a section about time travel in books, TV shows, and movies, but we're not done yet," he tells me.

"Awesome."

The nose-wrinkle frown has never been more pronounced. "I know you, man. You don't think it's awesome. Why would you worm your way into my basement to see our project? So you can dump on it? Does that make you feel good about blowing us off to work with Clarisse?"

"That's not it at all," I try to explain. "I *wanted* to see your project! And it's *good*! It's just that—"

He cuts me off. "What's with you, Mason? Ever since that sleepover, you've been weird. You won't work with me on the project. You're a jerk to Ava. You go out for football, which you *hate*! You're my best friend, and I don't even know you anymore!"

"That's because—" I bite my tongue. How can I tell him? If he thinks I'm weird now, what will he think when he hears the truth?

"I think you should go," Ty says in a quiet tone.

I back up a step. Mason Rolle, high school senior, is used to not being friends with Ty. That's the way it's been for five solid years. Still, in this twelve-year-old moment, this is shocking. Neither of us has ever kicked the other out of one of our houses before. I suddenly feel really sad.

Ty's voice is a little louder now. "I want you to leave."

The only good thing about what's happening is being friends with Ty again. And if I don't do something drastic, our friendship will be gone even sooner than it's supposed to be.

So I open my big mouth and it all comes pouring out. "The reason you don't know me is—it's not really me."

He snorts. "Yeah, right."

"I mean, it's *me*," I clarify, babbling a little. "But I'm not the same me. I'm me from the future."

He just stares.

"I *time traveled*! Not the way we always talked about, where you go back centuries. I'm seventeen years old. You're there too—everybody is, only older. We're high school seniors. I can't explain exactly how it happened, but I got into a really bad car wreck. And the next thing I knew, I was twelve again, waking up at that sleepover in the lab."

Anger suffuses his cheeks. "Is this supposed to be funny?"

"It sounds crazy, but you have to believe me!" I plead. "Everything we're doing, I did already, five years ago. Not exactly the same way, but a lot of it. How do you think I knew it was Dominic and Miggy who attacked us at the sleepover?"

He folds his arms in front of him. "So tell me about the future, since you've already been there. Are there flying cars? Do we live in a bio-dome on Pluto?"

"It's only five years, man. Things aren't that different."

He sticks out his jaw belligerently. "Tell me, future boy!"

I think hard. "You know that new app, TikTok—the one that's like YouTube, only too limited and nobody's ever going to use it? Well, by senior year, it's the biggest thing around."

"Thank goodness the future of humanity is safe," he comments sarcastically.

I go on. "Kobe Bryant is going to die in a freak helicopter crash in California. And a disease called coronavirus is going to shut down the whole world for over a year."

He rolls his eyes. "Too bad there's no way for me to check on any of this—or maybe that's the whole point."

I rack my brain. What will convince him? Something local. Something he's close to. I snap my fingers.

"You know that new music teacher, Mr. Nekomis? He and Ms. Alexander are going to get married."

"Get out!"

"Seriously!" I'm practically begging. "Just wait and see! I wouldn't lie to you. You think I'm happy about this? I'm losing my mind trying to figure out what happened to me and how to undo it!"

He turns his back on me and sets about straightening up the research for his project. I stand there a minute, but the message is clear. I'm being dismissed.

"I deserve better from you," I tell him. "You're my best friend."

"Oh, yeah?" he shoots back at me. "Are you talking about now or *senior year*?"

I start up the stairs. "You may not believe me, but you will. I never lied to you!"

As I let myself out the front door, it occurs to me that I *have* lied to Ty—when I broke our non-Ava treaty. Halfway across the lawn, I freeze, mind whirling. The first time I was twelve, our non-Ava treaty was already in force by this date. But this time around, we don't need a non-Ava treaty, because Ty's her friend and I'm not. So history is already changed. There are other changes too. I wasn't a football player, and I didn't partner with Clarisse, and I never met Madame Zeynab.

It makes me think of a diagram I saw in the research notes for the project in Ty's basement. It showed a time traveler, transported back to a moment in time, confronted with a decision. If he chose A, it would lead him through the life he'd led before. But if he chose B, he would be setting out in a new direction.

Every time I do something a little differently than before—whether it's avoiding Ava or teaching Rufus that Roto-Rooter trucks are bad—I'm that guy in the diagram, choosing B.

I stand there like a lawn ornament, with a growing sense that I'm on the threshold of uncovering something important, something meaningful. I picture the figure in the diagram, at the crossroads depicted by two hand-drawn arrows.

I remember Madame's words.

Two paths.

Two futures.

TWELVE YEARS OLD
OCTOBER 13

The Pasco Middle School Panthers are scheduled to play our first game—the annual grudge match against our archrivals, the Clara Barton Broncos this Saturday.

Sue me, I've made it all the way to senior year in this district and I never knew we even had an archrival, let alone that her name was Clara. The only team I was ever on was math, and the mathletes from Clara Barton were never a threat. They wouldn't know the difference between pi and pie.

All around the school, there are mannequins in Broncos jerseys, and we're encouraged to bombard them with wadded-up pieces of paper and other trash. This is a building where, if your candy wrapper lands so much as an eighth of an inch short of the lunch-room wastebasket, you get a detention. We don't just have to play the Broncos. We have to annihilate them. And the whole school seems to be on board with that. This, Coach Gallo explains at the pep rally on lucky Friday the thirteenth, is to teach us about sportsman-ship.

The pep rally is a pretty humiliating experience, because the players have to run out on the stage, looking ferocious, when our names are called. The biggest cheers go to the eighth graders, but a couple of seventh graders get big ovations too—like Dominic, who Coach introduces as the Dominator. When my turn comes—dead last—Coach Gallo bellows into the microphone, "Give it up for Mason 'the Spaceman' Rolle!"

It gets a confused chorus of "Who?" mixed with a lot of laughing from the seventh graders who know me. Coach means well, but how many times do I have to tell him that nickname is not a compliment?

The torture doesn't end there. It's a Panthers tradition that before the first game, all the football players get auctioned off for charity. Whoever "wins" you, you have to be that kid's butler for the entire day Monday. You have to carry their books, answer their phone, and be their waiter in the cafeteria.

It's supposed to be fun. But as the first few stars sell off in bidding wars of eighth-grade girls, it starts to sink in that nobody's going to bid on me. Not that I'm so keen on being somebody's servant. But I don't want to be the only Panther who gets no takers. I'm already the team joke, the backup to the backup to the backup. But I don't want to broadcast that in front of the entire school.

My one hope is that a couple of other players will be left on the shelf along with me. No such luck. The bidding isn't exactly furious, but every single kid before me gets snapped up. A week ago, I would have been confident that Ty would rescue me from being the designated loser. But he's mad at me now, because I told him the truth. And I'm mad at him for not believing me. I wouldn't want to be his butler anyway.

Coach Gallo calls my name, and I know exactly how this is going to go. There won't be any bids, and it's going to be crickets for a while. The more awkward it gets, the more people are going to start laughing. And finally some teacher is going to have mercy and bid a quarter on me, and I'm going to die of embarrassment right here on the stage.

And then, out of nowhere, a voice calls, "I bid five dollars for Mason!"

Every single head in the gym whips around to see who on earth would pay five bucks for the likes of me.

Coach Gallo thunders, "Sold!"

To the winning bidder: Ava Petrakis.

I'm going to be Ava's butler . . .

I replay that thought over and over again on the ride to Clara Barton Middle School. Why did Ava, of all people, make that bid? Why would she even want to? It's not as if I've been very nice to her since she got to Pasco.

And there's no getting my mind off the subject. I figured the ride would be loud and distracting, because football players are loud people. But the bus is so quiet that it's almost eerie. Everybody's so nervous about the game that they're clammed up, staring down at their phones.

The only Panther who isn't scared is me. Not that I have nerves of steel or anything like that. But before we clattered onto the bus, Coach Gallo pulled me aside.

"Listen, Rolle. You know I like you. But don't expect to get onto the field today."

I try to seem disappointed, but it's actually a huge relief. I get beaten up enough in practice. The last thing I need is to expose myself to the tender mercies of our archrivals in a grudge match.

To keep my mind off Ava and the butler thing, I'm the chattiest person on the bus, talking nonstop and finding memes on my phone to pass around.

"If you don't shut up," Dominic warns darkly, "you'll be having my cleats for your last meal."

Miggy pats him on the shoulder pads. "Take it easy, Dominator." To me, he adds, "Got to hand it to you, Spaceman. I don't know how you can stay so calm."

Coach Gallo's a good guy, but this is really his fault. This is what you get for convincing everybody that if we don't win this game, our school might as well be leveled to the ground by photon torpedoes.

I'm surprised at how full the bleachers are. Our fans from Pasco are the whole left section. I spot Mom, Dad, and Serena in the third row. I'm a little annoyed by that. They never got very rah-rah over the science fairs, math competitions, and chess tournaments

I'm usually involved in, but they came all this way to watch me ride the pine. Dad even brought a home-made sign that reads: GO MASON!!! Mom just looks worried. When I first told her I'd joined the Panthers, her only comment was: "But you'll get hurt!" How could I ever explain it? You can't be injured in a game you have zero chance of playing in.

I notice that they didn't bring Rufus, though, which might be a problem. Rufus doesn't like being left alone for too long. If this game goes into overtime, he could express his displeasure by making a statement on the living room carpet.

If you've never seen a middle school football game, it's not much like the NFL, with quarterbacks throwing sixty-yard bombs. If there is a pass, it's more like a three-yard pass to a guy you hope can break a few tackles. On most plays, there's a handoff and twenty-two players sort of trip over each other until somebody blows a whistle.

"It's all about blocking" is Coach Gallo's philosophy. It makes sense, because both teams have a few fast guys. If you can clear a path for one of them, he has a pretty good chance of running all the way for a touchdown.

That doesn't happen very often, though. So at the

end of the second quarter, we're down 8–6. Each team has scored one touchdown, but the Broncos made their two-point conversion and we muffed ours.

In the locker room at halftime, Coach Gallo is raving about how we're in striking distance, and how "we just need one guy to step up and make a play."

It rained last night, and I can't help noticing that every single player is smeared with mud and chunks of turf. All except me, that is. I look like I'm about to step into a photo shoot for the uniform company.

But here's the problem: Nobody steps up for either team. So as the third quarter ticks into the fourth, the score is still 8–6 in favor of Clara Barton. And the pressure for something—*anything*—to happen is building. Our fans get loud, encouraging us to score. Their fans get even louder, urging the Broncos to hold on to their razor-thin lead. I see my dad in the bleachers, waving the GO MASON!!! sign and cheering, with Mom trying to calm him down. I think Serena might be asleep.

As the wet field gets torn up even more, every tackle becomes a mud bath. Tempers run short; arguments flare up.

Then the game breaks wide open. On fourth down, our quarterback tears himself free and scampers all the way to the goal line before the Broncos wrestle him to the ground. A shoving match erupts as the refs try to figure out whether he made it into the end zone. When the dust clears, the ruling is no score, and Clara Barton takes over the ball at the half-yard line. Our guys freak out, because there's less than a minute to play, so we're almost definitely going to lose. Three of our best eighth graders are ejected. It gets so rowdy that Coach Gallo has to run onto the field and pull Dominic clear of the fray before he gets thrown out too.

On the sidelines, during the time-out, the coach pleads with us to keep our cool.

"But Coach," Miggy wails, "if the Broncos make one first down, it's game over!"

There's a babble of agonized agreement.

Coach Gallo waves his arms for quiet. "We need to shut them down and get the ball back! But we've got no chance if we can't focus! I like intensity, but not if you let yourself get so wild that you can't do your job! Look at Rolle here! You don't see him losing control!"

My beat up, bone-weary, dirt-smeared teammates take in my immaculate jersey beneath my clean face and spotless helmet that gleams in the afternoon sun.

"Yeah, look at Rolle!" The Dominator is bitter.

"He's keeping control because he knows there's no chance in a million that he's ever going to play in this game!"

And even though Coach told me the exact same thing as we were getting on the bus this morning, somehow hearing it from one of his players makes him blow his stack.

"What are you talking about, Holyoke?" he bellows, his red face moving into the purple range. "We're a team! *Everybody* contributes! Get your butt out there, Rolle! Left corner! Let's get this ball back while there's still time!"

That's how I make my football debut—in the last minute of a grudge match, with my team needing a miracle.

The crowd is an uninterrupted roar. I glance over at the stands. My father is gripping his homemade sign so tightly that he's mangling it. My mother's worried look has been ratcheted up to the level of raw fear. Besides me, she knows better than anybody how little I belong out here.

Dominic calls the defense into a huddle. "All right, guys. We're a man short"—I think he means me—"so everybody has to step up."

I'm a little offended, but I don't argue with him. I

can't. My throat has seized shut, leaving me incapable of speech.

On the first two plays, the Dominator breaks free of his blocker and drops the ball carrier after only a short gain. It's third down and seven, which means the Broncos have to pass if they have any hope of getting a first down. Our players are shouting at the sideline, begging Coach Gallo to pull me out. I have never been so terrified in my entire life. All game long, the coach could have put me in at any moment and, chances are, I wouldn't have done much harm—until right now. A cornerback isn't very important on a short run. But against a pass, he's vital.

Before Coach can react, the Broncos snap the ball. The quarterback sidesteps a diving tackle from Dominic, cocks his arm, and lets fly. The ball sails through a forest of reaching hands. But it's a little behind the receiver, who can't get himself turned around in time. The pass bounces off his shoulder pads and spins in a high arc—directly into my hands.

I'm so amazed that I caught it—it never happens in practice—that I just stand there, staring at the muddy football wrapped in my arms. It's like I'm so astonished to have the ball that I've forgotten what comes next.

"Run!!" screams a chorus of Panther voices.

The shrieks of the crowd resounding in my ears, I make it three shaky, unathletic steps before the biggest, toughest eighth grader on the Broncos slams into me with the force of a battering ram.

I go one way; the ball goes another. I hit the turf in a cascade of mud and roll over just in time to see Miggy scoop up my fumble and throw himself over the goal line for the winning touchdown.

Final score 12–8, Pasco.

I get the game ball. It's really muddy.

"It washes off, Spaceman." Miggy laughs gleefully. "Ever heard of water?"

He's kidding. Miggy isn't mad at all that he scored the winning touchdown, but the game ball went to me. He's kind of a nicer person than I always thought he was.

I'm pretty thrilled with myself. Sure, I get that I'm not exactly a star. I only made one catch—and when I fumbled, it was pure luck that the ball went to Miggy. But if I hadn't made that interception, we wouldn't have won.

It's a joyous locker room. We had all made our peace with the fact that we were going to lose to the hated

Clara Barton. But thanks to a play by the worst person on the team—the backup to the backup to the backup—that didn't happen.

Only Dominic has a sour face as we load ourselves and our gear back onto the bus. "Goofiest game I ever played in. First a pick, then a fumble, then a scoop-and-score. And thanks to a guy who wouldn't know football from go fish!"

"Dude," Miggy reminds him, "we *won*."

"I'd rather lose than win by dumb luck."

"The pick was one hundred percent legit," Rolando points out. "Spaceman could have dropped it. He didn't."

"Because it fell into his arms," Dominic growls. "If it had hit him in the mouth, he would have swallowed it!"

I guess the Dominator doesn't like dominating unless he's the one doing the domination. If anybody else contributes, it's no good—especially when it's me.

Coach Gallo has no patience for that attitude. "Wipe that scowl off your face, Holyoke. We win as a team; we lose as a team. Today we got the dub. That's all that matters."

The driver closes the door, and the victorious Panthers roar off toward home. As we exit the parking lot, our fans line the roadway and give us a big cheer. Dad is punching the air with what's left of the GO MASON sign. Mom looks like she just remembered what Rufus does when you leave him alone for too long. I make a mental note to clean the carpet and give Dad credit for it. If that won't win him points, nothing will.

We pound at the windows and wave down at our families and friends. I never understood the big deal everybody makes about sports, but I have to admit that, even if I make it back to my seventeen-year-old life, today is a day I'll never forget.

None of us are on our phones for the fifteen-minute ride home. The bus resounds with the clamor of voices replaying every down of the game. I even join in, although my only highlight is "Suddenly, the ball was there—and I caught it!"

The bus enters Pasco and starts along the main drag toward school. I glance out the flyspecked window and my celebration comes to an abrupt end.

It's Madame Zeynab's Crystal Ball and Tearoom—at least it used to be. The faded awning is gone. So are the hanging beads in the doorway. The tarot cards in the window have been replaced by a cardboard sign, hand-lettered STORE FOR RENT, followed by a phone number.

Madame Zeynab? Gone? *No!* I *need* her! She's the only person who can explain what's happening to me!

"Hey, check it out!" Miggy points. "The witch lady went out of business!"

"Spaceman must have scared her out of town," Dominic rumbles.

For all I know, he's right. Was it something she saw in me that made her pull up stakes and disappear?

When a professional psychic reads your palm and heads for the hills, you know it's time to hit the panic button.

TWELVE YEARS OLD
OCTOBER 16

At the sound of the doorbell Monday morning, I feel a surge of happiness.

Ty's back!

We've barely said three words to each other since he threw me out last week, and we haven't texted at all. I've started punching his number into my phone at least fifteen times, only to chicken out before placing the call.

I can't get downstairs fast enough. But when I throw the door open with a hearty "Hey, man—" who's standing there beaming at me but Ava.

"Hi, butler!"

"What are you doing here?" I blurt.

She gives me all the teeth. "You *work* for me, remember? You have to carry my backpack to school."

The auction! In all the excitement of the football game and the horrible news about Madame Zeynab disappearing, I totally forgot that I have to be Ava's butler.

I guess I never really thought about what that meant. Oh, sure, I figured the football players would get ordered around at lunch a little, like our "employers" would make us go for chips and ice cream bars. I didn't think it was going to be a full day of service.

I grab my own stuff and join her outside. As I throw her backpack over my free shoulder, I practically drop to the ground. "What have you got in here—bricks?"

"Yeah, it's kind of heavy," she admits. "It's a wallpaper roll of spinning clock hands. It's for—"

"I know what it's for," I cut her off, starting down the walk. I take big steps so I won't have to talk to her.

No such luck. She catches up anyway and she's

determined to make conversation. "When I bid on you, I didn't realize I was going to get the hero of the whole football game."

"I'm not the hero," I tell her stubbornly. "I fumbled. That's like the worst thing you can do. It was pure luck that Miggy picked up the ball and scored."

She shrugs. "If it wasn't for you, we would have lost. That's what people are saying."

"I didn't think you'd care about football," I put in. "You being a big science kid and all that."

"It's possible to like science and other things too," she lectures me. "Sports are really just science, you know. Take a home run. It's the speed of the ball, and the speed of the bat, and the distance to the fence . . ."

I've tuned her out because I see Ty approaching from the rear, coming up fast. There's no actual steam puffing out of his ears, but I can tell from his posture that he's ticked off that I'm with Ava, who he wants all to himself. No matter how hard I try to do everything differently from last time, it always ends up the same—Ava and me, me and Ava, with Ty jealous and angry.

I speak first, before Ty can start yelling at me. "It's not my fault. I have no choice. I'm her butler."

"Yeah, I hear you're a football star now," Ty says,

almost like it's an insult. "Congratulations."

Ty tries to pull Ava's pink backpack off my shoulder, but she stops him. "That's not how it works," she explains. "Mason has to carry it. It's his *job*."

The smile never leaves her face. She obviously has no clue that we're both on the verge of throwing punches. She's so well-meaning and flat-out *nice* that she can't imagine us fighting over her. It's just like last time, when the two of us needed a whole treaty about her. And here we are again!

"But we've got work to do on our project," Ty complains.

She unzips the backpack and hands him the giant wallpaper roll. I immediately stand up a lot straighter.

"You get started on the display," she tells him. "I'll catch up with you later. How often am I ever going to get to have my own butler? I'm not going to waste a minute of it."

Ty scrambles to keep pace with us, fuming over the wallpaper.

Ava might have unwittingly ruined my life, but one thing I can't accuse her of is being unprepared. She's thought a lot about how today is going to go. "I've only got a butler for one day," she explains. "So I have to make the most of it. I call it the MLP—Maximum Labor Plan."

"You mean Maximum Humiliation Plan," I retort.

"There's nothing humiliating about doing the job you've agreed to do," she lectures as we walk into the school. "Honest work is empowering."

Task one is cleaning out her locker.

I always thought of girls as much neater than guys. I think it came from the time in elementary school when Dominic and Miggy shoved Ty and me inside the girls' bathroom and we realized how much less disgusting it was than the boys'. But Ava's locker is a dumpster.

"I'm a slob," she admits with a mixture of embarrassment and a kind of defiant pride. "Every project I get back, every paper—I don't take the time to make a place for it. I'm too anxious to move on to the next thing. So I just jam it in there and force the door shut. And after a few weeks—well, you see the end product."

I sneeze from a faceful of dust. "Got it."

So I pull out all her junk, forming a mini-mountain on the floor. Next, I wipe down the locker with rubbing alcohol, which she brought from home—another reason why the backpack was so heavy.

As the opening bell approaches, every kid in Pasco Middle School gets to see me on my hands and knees, sweating over Ava's locker. And every single one of them has a comment to make about it. I'm tempted to squeeze myself into the locker, close the door behind me, and wait to die from the alcohol fumes.

The other football players are the worst. "That's why he's Spaceman," Dominic comments loudly at the sight of my hind end sticking out of Ava's locker. "Because his butt points to outer space!"

"Keep scrubbing!" Miggy encourages me. "Put some back into it!"

"Your turn will come," I warn him. "You're a butler, too, remember?"

He shrugs. "Brittany gave me a pass. Nobody takes it seriously, you know. Just Ava. It helps to hook a big sucker like you."

Clarisse shoots me a resentful look that I can't quite read. Maybe she's ticked off that I'm not working on our infinity mirror. But considering that she wouldn't let me touch it from day one, I don't know why she'd start complaining now.

"Good work," Ava praises me. "Now put it all back."

I take in the pile on the floor. "But it's just a bunch of old homework, and pop quizzes, and review sheets.

What do you need it for?"

"If good grades are worth the effort," she explains, "so is keeping the rewards of all my hard work."

I can vouch for the good grades. I mean, Ty and I are pretty smart, but Ava is wall-to-wall A-pluses. She even gets extra points for neatness, which we never do. She's that rare student who's just as beloved by the other kids as she is by her teachers.

You can learn a lot about a person by the contents of her locker. For example, Ava has no movie star or teen heartthrob photos in there. Instead, she has pictures of famous scientists, like Galileo and Albert Einstein. She has a labeled diagram of a DNA double helix, a pamphlet on starting your own alpaca farm, and a menu from a New York City restaurant called TNT.

"It was my favorite place," she explains, her blue-green eyes far away. "Their mild sauce is hotter than everybody else's hot sauce, their hot sauce is hotter than everybody else's blazing; and their thermonuclear sauce has been banned in seventeen states."

Answering Ava's phone is another one of my responsibilities. I figured that wouldn't be an issue during the school day, but no. She has too many friends, and she's arranged with somebody to call during every single class change. Whenever I hear her ringtone—the opening chords of "New York, New York"—I have to answer, "Ava's phone, Mason the butler speaking, service with a smile. How may I direct you?"

Lunch is Ava's finest hour, condensed to twenty-four minutes. She's brought a linen tablecloth, a bud vase with a yellow rose, and a candle that Assistant Principal Grabenstein won't let me light. She even has a little silver bell that she rings very delicately when she requires service—which is about every fifteen seconds. She sends me running for napkins, ketchup packets, salt, an extra chocolate milk, a pat of butter, a macadamia-nut cookie, and a replacement for her fruit cup, which has a hair in it.

We are the center of attention in the cafeteria. You can hear a pin drop, except when Ava rings that little bell. That brings on a thunderous ovation.

I'm embarrassed, but I feel something else too—*special*. When Coach Gallo read out my name during the auction, no one had any idea who I was, but everybody sure knows me now. The next time Ava rings for me, I take a bow and the lunchroom resounds with cheers. I have no idea why, but for some reason, I'm having more fun than I've had ever since I woke up in the lab and found myself twelve again. It might be the most fun I've had going back all the way to when I was twelve the first time. One thing that's true in both timelines: Ava is really something.

There's a chorus of boos when lunch is over. I'm not sure I want it to end, either. As I escort Ava out of the cafeteria, my teammates on the Panthers line up and high-five me, even the eighth graders. A few of them had to do a handful of butler-y things, but I was the star of the show—thanks to Ava.

When the final bell rings at three thirty, I figure I'm off the hook. Guess again. Ava makes me carry her backpack to the edge of school property. I almost give her an argument, but what's the point?

When we reach the road, she slips the pink bag over her own shoulder. "Thanks for today, Mason. You were a really good sport."

My first impulse is to exclaim: *Are you kidding? It was the best day ever!*

But I can't say that. Ty is about forty feet away on the sidewalk, and if looks could kill, I'd be a little pile of ash on the cement. Besides, I have to stick to my purpose, which is to avoid what happened between Ava and me the first time around. Today was a wake-up call. I don't have a crush on her like last time—I'm still seventeen inside. But there's something about her—it's impossible not to like her. I can't let my guard down when it comes to keeping my distance.

So I mumble, "Whatever," and jog back toward the field house for football practice.

Coach Gallo makes a point of telling me that, even though my interception helped us get the win against Clara Barton, I shouldn't expect any more playing time going forward.

I'm not insulted. I'm still the smallest, the slowest, the weakest, and the worst. Still, there's a subtle change in the air. I'm one of the guys now. I *belong* on this team.

Dominic is the only player who doesn't think so. "Can't you take a hint, Spaceman? Nobody wants you on the Panthers."

It hurts, but not a single voice in the locker room backs him up. That has to count as progress.

After practice, I come out of the field house to find Clarisse waiting for me. She's got the same aggrieved expression she's been wearing all day.

I take a stab at the reason behind it. "I know," I tell her. "I haven't exactly been pulling my weight on our science-fair project."

But that's not what's on her mind. "How come everybody loves Ava and nobody likes me?" she blurts suddenly.

"What are you talking about? Everybody likes you!"

"No, they don't," she says sadly. "Not the way they like *her*. It's not fair. I've lived in this town my whole life. She shows up and, five minutes later, the whole school's eating out of her hand."

"That's not true," I protest.

"Oh, yeah? How about the way you followed her around like an adoring puppy all day?"

I try to laugh. "That was my *job*. The charity auction thing."

"You were loving it," she accuses.

Uh-oh. I hope Ava didn't notice.

"But it's not just you," Clarisse presses on. "Ty is in love with her. The other girls all want to hang out with her. She's friends with Emma and Kennedy and that whole crowd. Even Dominic, Miggy, Austin, the popular guys—they can't wait for her to ditch Ty so she can join the beautiful people. Why her and not me?"

"You hate those people," I remind her. "You wouldn't want to be a part of that crew anyway."

"Don't change the subject," she admonishes me. "What is it about Ava? What's she got that I don't?"

She has a point. Ava and Clarisse are actually a lot alike. Off the top of my head, I'm tempted to say Clarisse is a little obsessed with school stuff. Thinking back to the contents of Ava's locker, though—the way she keeps every homework assignment and quiz—the two of them are pretty similar. Straight-A students. Science kids.

But when I was twelve—legit twelve—I had a crush on Ava probably before I even knew it. And Clarisse, who I've known all my life—no crush, no nothing. And now that I'm looking at it with seventeen-year-old eyes, I know that Ty and I didn't treat her right. When kids made fun of us and called us dweebs, she always stuck up for us. When Dominic and Miggy and other bullies targeted us, she got right in their faces, even though she understood that she'd be targeted too. She should have been one of our best friends—smart, supportive, and absolutely fearless! And what did she get from us? Ignored.

I see it. I just can't explain it.

Clarisse interprets my silence as stalling. "I should have known better than to try to talk about this with you. As if you have any clue how it feels to be me."

"What's that supposed to mean?" I picture myself through eighth grade, through high school, enemies with Ty, alienated from Ava. Through losing my dog and my parents splitting up—if there's ever stuff you don't want to go through alone, it's that. Yeah, I know how it feels to be her, on the outside looking in.

"You heard me," she snaps back. "What would you know about it? The big football star. You're almost as popular as Ava!"

I laugh out loud at that one. It's the wrong thing to do. Enraged, Clarisse storms away.

I follow her. "I wasn't making fun of you! It's just that I *stink* at football!"

She breaks into a run. I speed up too, following her across the schoolyard. "Come on, Clarisse! Don't be like that!"

The next thing I know, I'm running flat out just to keep pace with her. These past weeks of football practice have gotten me in the best shape of my life, and still she's pulling away from me.

I stare after her. There's always been an awkwardness to Clarisse, a stiffness to her motion, almost like her entire body is magnetically charged, and she's attracting and repelling herself at the same time. But when she runs, she's a different person. Her long legs fall into an open, easy stride. She's relaxed, graceful, and— I realize as I fall farther and farther behind—super fast. She's a natural. It's the only thing she's natural at!

If I can play a sport I'm no good at and have zero interest in, then maybe . . .

Since I'm never going to catch up with her, I have to find another way to capture her attention. I trip myself up on purpose, hit the ground like a ton of bricks, and roll twenty feet before I come to a shuddering halt.

A moment later, she's standing over me, as I knew she would be. That's something to like about Clarisse— she's a good person. I don't know if I appreciated it the first time I was twelve, but I do now.

"Mason, are you okay?" She isn't even breathing hard.

"You"—I gasp, struggling for air—"are going out for the track team!"

She's bewildered. "Why would I? I don't care about sports."

"Trust me."

TWELVE YEARS OLD
OCTOBER 19

Another thing I forgot about my old life—how annoying it is to try to make a phone call when Rufus is around.

Basically, the sheepdog can't stand the fact that you're paying attention to something other than him. So he does everything in his power to distract you. And his power, as I've mentioned, is not small.

First he tries the affection angle, licking my face as I struggle to hold the phone to my ear. I can barely hear over the licking and slobbering.

"Get out of here!" I hiss, shoving him away. "This is important!"

I'm on hold with the real estate company that's trying to rent out Madame Zeynab's old store. I got the number from the sign in the tea-shop window. It's the only clue I have that might help me reconnect with the fortune-teller. I've got to find out what she knows about me—about my "two futures," as she put it.

Rufus starts in on some insulted whining, but when that doesn't get enough of a rise from me, he turns up the volume to a full-throated howl. Next comes the *whack-whack-whack* of Dad downstairs, banging on the ceiling with a broomstick. Uh-oh—this always knocks down little pieces of popcorn plaster, which makes my mother furious. I've got to find a way to shut up my dog.

So I sit cross-legged on the carpet and pat my lap invitingly. Rufus leaps aboard, knocking me flat. By the time the receptionist comes on the line, I'm buried under 120 pounds of dog.

"Sir, are you still there?"

My first response is muffled by a mouthful of fur, but I'm able to wrestle myself free enough to exclaim, "Yes! I'm here!"

"The only forwarding information I have for that

address is a company called Rappaport Holdings," the woman informs me.

I'm devastated. "That's not right! This person is an old lady! Madame Zeynab!"

Rufus's stomach lets out a loud gurgle in sympathy with my complaint.

"I beg your pardon, sir?"

"Are you totally sure?" I plead.

"Not at all sure," the receptionist replies. "But it's the only number I have. Would you like it?"

I've lost my notepad, so I have to write the number on my arm. Rufus finds this fascinating and tries to lick at it, smudging the ink.

A quick Google search confirms what I already suspected: There is no such company as Rappaport Holdings in Pasco or anywhere around here.

So I don't have much hope when I try the number.

I wait through eleven rings, and then a voice-mail message begins to play: *"Hi, you've reached Zelda. Leave a message at the beep."*

Zelda? Who's Zelda?

At school, I'm still doing my best to avoid Ava. It's going so-so.

On the plus side, I don't have to be her butler

anymore. But after such a great day, it's almost impossible to go back to being cold to her. That leaves avoiding her, which is hard, considering we're in the same homeroom and several of the same classes.

"Oh, wow!" she exclaims. "This looks cool!"

She's pointing at a new poster on the school's main bulletin board. By new, I mean new to her. I've seen it before—five years ago. It's advertising Harvest Festival, which begins on October 28.

The sucking sound I hear is my heart sinking below my abdomen. It's happening again. I knew it would, but I'm still not ready.

"It's boring," I say quickly. "I wouldn't be caught dead in that dump." For example, right behind the Tilt-A-Whirl when the storm hits.

She's drinking in the details under DON'T MISS on the poster. "Will there really be a pumpkin that weighs as much as a Mini Cooper?"

"Who cares?" I sneer. "It's all for little kids." But I can tell she's hooked. No matter what I say, she's determined to love this, just like last time. So I add, "You should go with Ty. He's a huge Harvest Festival fan."

"But you just said it's lousy," she teases.

"For *me*," I explain, inventing rapidly. "I'm a football

player. We hate everything. But Ty doesn't play football—"

She smirks at me. "You know what I think? You're
all talk. I think I'll see you there."

I feel like I'm on a high-diving platform, and my
one ambition is to chicken out and retreat down the
stairs. But my feet have just left the board, and I'm
already on my way over and out. The pool is still far
away, but at this point, there's no going back. I'd need
wings, and I don't have them.

No. I won't let it happen. Not again.

Clarisse update: She makes the track team, big surprise. Her tryout times set school records for the 200
and 400 meters. She's by far the fastest on the squad,
including the eighth graders.

A normal person would be happy about that. Not
Clarisse.

"I only tried out because you made me."

"I didn't make you," I defend myself.

"You said people would like me. They don't like me.
They hate me because I'm faster than them. People
who didn't even hate me *before*."

"It's going to work," I insist. "Trust me."

"I already trusted you and look where it got me," she complains. "Now I've got no time to work on our science-fair project."

I can help with that. Now that Clarisse is spending her afternoons on the track, she's willing to accept my input on our infinity mirror.

An infinity mirror is an optical illusion formed by placing two mirrors opposite each other. The outer-most unit has to be only partially reflective, so you can see through it. If you set the two pieces inside a shadow box with some LED lights between them, those lights will be reflected to infinity. It's pretty cool, because it looks like you're gazing into an endless void, even though the whole setup is only a few inches thick.

I get the idea to make it look like a window into outer space. "We can set up a fake telescope in front of it. And we'll use white pinpoint lights to be the stars. And at the center of the telescope glass, we can put a tiny picture of a famous object in astronomy—like that first-ever photo of a black hole."

Clarisse frowns at me. "Nobody's ever taken a picture of a black hole."

Oops—she's right. It's only seventh grade—that

picture won't exist for another two years! I've got to watch myself.

We finally decide to use the most distant object in the known universe, a galaxy called MACS0647-JD. Not a catchy name like Andromeda or the Milky Way, but this thing is 13.3 billion light-years away.

We squint at the image of it on the internet—a tiny reddish dot among so many other dots. The light from that galaxy is 13.3 billion years old by the time it reaches us here on Earth. If that's not time travel, what is?

I'm finally going to hand in the time-travel project that I messed up weeks in the past and years in the future.

I spend the rest of the day racking my brain over how to avoid Harvest Festival. My main idea is this: I don't have to miss the whole five days. I just have to get out of the first night. I know something nobody else does. The storm is going to do so much damage that they cancel the rest of the fair. Skip the opening, and I'm in the clear.

During my first shot at being twelve, I tried to tell Ava I had family plans. Back then I couldn't make it stick because it was all a lie. That's how she broke down my resistance.

But what if we make real family plans—something rock solid that I can't get out of no matter what?

"When's the last time we visited Grandma and Grandpa?" I ask Mom on the phone as I make my way to the field house for football practice. "I miss them. I think we should go visit next weekend. Not *this* weekend," I add quickly. "You know, the weekend that includes Saturday, October twenty-eighth."

"Don't you have a football game that day?" she asks.

"We can leave *after* the game," I reason. As in after the game, but before Harvest Festival.

"It wouldn't be worth it," she decides. "We'd get there late and have to leave after lunch the next day. That's not a visit. Besides, you'll miss the opening of Harvest Festival."

"I hate Harvest Festival."

"No, you don't."

"I outgrew it a long time ago," I insist.

"Well, Serena didn't. You can take her."

Something I always used to tell Ty comes back to me: *You're lucky to be an only child.* It's never been more true than right now.

"And you can still enjoy the fireworks," Mom goes on. "Everyone loves fireworks."

"They get canceled," I blurt. "I mean they *would* get canceled. You know, if the weather was bad."

She's losing patience. "We'll see Grandma and Grandpa at Thanksgiving. To be honest, Mason, I don't relish the idea of six hours in your father's car. He swears he doesn't smoke in it, but it smells like a stale ashtray. And after a long drive, we all will."

I step into the field house, totally defeated.

My status with the football players has improved five hundred percent, but that's only like being promoted from microbe to ant. Most of the time, the eighth graders ignore the seventh graders like we don't even exist. And even among the seventh graders, I'm the backup to the backup to the backup. Then there's Dominic, who hates my guts, period. So I'm not too big on speaking up in the locker room.

But this is an emergency. "Hey, guys!" I pipe up, self-conscious that my voice sounds higher than most of the other players'. "What's everybody doing after the game on October twenty-eighth?"

They turn bewildered eyes in my direction. I think some of the eighth graders are trying to remember who I am. Anyway, nobody answers. A moment later, the locker room chatter resumes.

Miggy beckons me over. "What was that about, Spaceman? Nobody knows what they're going to be doing on the twenty-eighth. I don't know what I'm doing five minutes after practice."

"Isn't that the first night of Harvest Festival?" Austin puts in.

"You mean Doofus Festival," the Dominator announces at top volume.

"Exactly!" I hate to agree with Dominic, but it's the perfect setup. "We're way too old for that boring fair with the kiddie rides. So let's make a plan to blow it off and do something cool."

"Shut up, Spaceman!" The Dominator changes his tune. "Harvest Festival may stink, but it doesn't stink worse than you!"

I've got an audience now, among the seventh graders anyway. I can tell that at least a few of them kind of like Harvest Festival. But they can't admit that now that everybody's dumping on it.

"What have you got in mind?" Miggy asks me.

That's when I draw a blank, because I haven't thought that far ahead. So I say, "I don't know. But we have to come up with something. Otherwise, our parents will rope us into taking our little brothers and sisters and going on all the baby rides."

Honestly, anything that keeps me away from Ava is fine by me. We could go straight from the football game to shovel out Pasco Stables for all I care. Just so long as I can tell her that I'm not going to Harvest Festival because I have a team plan.

TWELVE YEARS OLD

OCTOBER 21

Mom and Serena take a pass on the Panthers' next football game. I'm not insulted. Sports aren't Mom's thing, and keeping Rufus from laying waste to the living room is. As for my sister, "I'd rather go hot-tubbing in lava" is her explanation.

Dad is there, minus the sign. I guess he's figured out my role as the backup to the backup to the backup. It's hard to root for a guy who never plays.

Because it's a home game, a lot more kids come to

cheer for the Panthers. For some reason, that makes me a little more self-conscious about my bench-warming duties. I don't think I belong on the field—or that it would even be healthy for me to be out there. But I have kind of a reputation now. I was Ava's butler. Not that butlering has anything to do with football, but still.

Speaking of Ava, she's at the game too, sitting between Ty and Clarisse on the bleachers. It's hard to see clearly from the field, but Ty looks a little smug for my taste. That means he's loving it that I'm the team nobody, riding the pine. From the way he keeps pointing at me on the sidelines, I can tell that he's making sure Ava notices it too.

We run up an easy 27–6 lead over our opponents, Athens Middle School. Coach Gallo calls it a "great team effort"—although he might just be happy that we're dominating, unlike last week, when everybody was sure we were going to lose until the very last whistle.

The coach is in such a good mood that he even puts me in the game in the fourth quarter, once we're too far ahead for me to mess it up. He acts like he's doing me a big favor, despite the fact that I'd much rather stay on the sidelines where it's safe. But I feel better about it when I see the scowl on Ty's face in the stands.

Now he can't call me a total benchwarmer. I take my position at cornerback with a new sense of purpose.

I don't expect to star, obviously, or even play acceptably well. But looking like a clown in front of everybody I know is definitely to be avoided.

It goes wrong on the very first snap. The guy I'm covering catches a pass, and I'm trying to tackle him but I slip. The next thing I know, I'm flat on my face on the grass, and this giant cleat comes stomping down on my butt. A shadow passes over me like when you're near the airport and a big plane comes in for a landing. A split second later the guy hits the ground three yards downfield and the play is over.

"Great tackle, Rolle!" Coach Gallo praises me.

Dominic is outraged. "What tackle? He fell down and the kid tripped over him!"

But the other Panthers think it's hilarious—especially the perfect shoeprint on the left cheek of my football pants. I have to take their word for it, since I can't see it. When Coach isn't looking, Rolando sneaks back to the locker room for his phone to take a picture of it.

The game ends pretty soon after that. In the crowd of spectators leaving the field, Dad waves at me and even manages to look proud. Great actor, my father.

Ty has a sour expression on his face. I made a tackle,

even if it was by accident. In my football career, that counts as exceeding expectations.

He hangs back, but the girls come over to congratulate me.

"That was good," Clarisse says. It's more a question than a statement of fact. "Right?"

"Sort of," I reply, rubbing my sore butt cheek. "My job was to get the guy down. It doesn't matter how it happened."

"Amazing game," Ava declares. "Hey, there's Austin! Great touchdown today!" She runs off, high-fiving her way through the team.

In the locker room, I don't get a game ball, since a tackle isn't as important as an interception. But I feel good about the fact that I contributed again, even if all I really did is get stomped on and tripped over.

Coach explains it to me. "It isn't about game balls and talent. It's about finding a way to help your team. And somehow you always do."

Dominic doesn't like that. He hates me so much that he's already announced that he refuses to be a part of hanging out with the team after next week's game. He's started talking about how great Harvest Festival is and how he's looking forward to it. I'm against it, so he has to be for it. Suddenly, it isn't Doofus Festival anymore.

It worries me a little, because the Dominator has a lot of influence over the seventh graders on the Panthers. And the team hangout can't fall through. When I mentioned it to Ava, the first thing she did was check with Miggy to make sure I wasn't making it up. At this point, she's so well liked around school that I can forget trying to put anything over on her. That's something I didn't realize during my first crack at seventh grade. I was too *out* to realize how *in* Ava already was.

Another problem is that there *is* no team plan other than the fact that we're planning one. So far, the only ideas are:

1) Team dinner at Buffalo Wild Wings
2) Go to a movie
3) Bowling

I see kids glancing over at Dominic as he raves about how awesome this year's Harvest Festival is going to be. Like New Year's Eve, the Fourth of July, and Mardi Gras all rolled into one, times a million.

It gives me a sinking feeling.

In the meantime, I've made zero progress in my effort to track down Madame Zeynab. My one clue is still that phone number for Rappaport Holdings, the one that brings up the voice-mail greeting from a woman named Zelda. I'm ninety-nine percent sure it's a wrong number, but I've started leaving messages on the off chance that this Zelda person might know something about how to reach the real Rappaport Holdings—and that the company could maybe put me in touch with Madame Zeynab. It's a long shot, but it's all I've got.

"Hi—uh—Zelda. You don't know me, but my name is Mason Rolle, and I'm looking for Madame Zeynab, who ran the fortune-telling shop in Pasco. She probably doesn't remember me, but I'm the kid with two futures. I really have to know what that means, so it's urgent that I get in touch with her—"

The doorbell rings as I'm leaving my fifth message of the week, and Rufus starts barking the house down. So I stammer out my number and hang up. Zelda is either the busiest person on the face of the earth, or she's deliberately ignoring me. She probably thinks I'm a stalker. And I'm pretty sure my voice is becoming increasingly desperate as my messages continue to go unanswered.

"Quiet, Rufus!" I toss over my shoulder as I head for the door. I fling it wide. Standing there is the last person I expect to see.

Ty.

We stare at each other for a few long awkward seconds. For an instant, I'm seventeen again, face-to-face with a kid I haven't been friends with for five long years. I have to remind myself that I'm not seventeen; I'm twelve, and Ty is my best friend. We've hit some bumps in the road since Ava showed up, and it definitely didn't help when he kicked me out of his house. But this is Ty. We're closer than family.

Wordlessly, I invite him in. Without hesitation, he heads straight for my room upstairs. Obviously, we have something to discuss. As always, we sit on the floor. That's another advantage of being twelve over seventeen. Furniture is unnecessary. You just flop down wherever you happen to be. Rufus joins us, looking anxiously from me to Ty and back again. He can tell that something's not quite right.

"What?" I say finally.

Ty looks like he's carrying the weight of the world on his shoulders. "Leaving school today, I saw Ms. Alexander and Mr. Nekomis in the parking lot." He looks up at me, his eyes haunted. "They were holding hands!"

Relief floods over me. "So it's started."

"Yeah, but how did you *know*?" he demands. "You said they were going to get married!"

"They are, but not till we're in high school," I explain. "They date for a long time."

"Stop doing that!" he explodes.

Rufus lets out a nervous whine. Conflict puts him on edge.

"Listen," I say. "When I told you how I know these things, you kicked me out of your house. So I'm not going to repeat it, because I don't want to get into a big stink. You can't kick me out of here. I live here."

"So it's true? You're really"—Ty's voice drops to a whisper—"*seventeen*?"

I try to be as honest as I can be. "Right now, I'm twelve, just like you. This body"—I tap my chest—"is no older than yours. But a month and a half ago, I was a senior in high school. I was taller, my voice was deeper, and my mom's Volkswagen was my car." I stretch out my arms. "All this—this life—is something I lived through and remember from five years ago. I have no idea why I'm back here, living it again. I think it might be because of the car accident."

He doesn't say anything for a long time. I don't know if he believes me, because a story like that has to be pretty hard to swallow. But I think he's accepted the fact that *I* believe me—that I'm telling him the truth as I see it. And even though I could be delusional, there's the truth about Ms. Alexander and Mr. Nekomis—and what explanation could there possibly be for that?

"What am I like?" he asks. "You know—in the future?"

I hesitate. I have to watch what I say. If I let slip that we're enemies, he's going to want to know what happened. "You're pretty much the same as you are now, only older. You're taller. Your hair's shorter." I hope he doesn't put two and two together and figure out that the reason I have so little to say about seventeen-year-old Ty is that the two of us are practically strangers. "You've got a good shot at class valedictorian." I don't mention that the reason Ty's the favorite is because I'm expelled.

"What about—Ava?" Ty inquires shyly.

I choose my words carefully. "She still goes to our school, but we're not that close to her anymore." He looks disappointed, and I keep talking in order to change the subject away from her. "We're both still into time travel, though." *We practically try to beat each other to death with dueling science-fair projects on the topic, but the only casualty is Mrs. Nekomis.*

"What else should I know?" he probes eagerly.

"Probably nothing," I reply. "If you have too much advance warning about what's coming, you might act differently and change the future." Big talk from me—I'm already tweaking my life a dozen ways.

Ty accepts this—the result of our endless conversations about time travel. But understandably, he wants more. "There must be something you can tell me."

"It's not all good," I admit sadly. "My folks split up in a couple of years. And Rufus"—I'm almost afraid to say it with my beloved sheepdog right there listening—"gets killed chasing a Roto-Rooter truck."

Ty is horrified. "No! Not Rufus!"

The sheepdog looks up at the sound of his name, but soon goes back to rolling a dust bunny across the carpet with his nose.

Ty's expression shifts slightly, from shock to worry. I can read his mind—if bad things can happen to the Rolles, they can happen to the Ehrlichs too.

"Your family is all fine," I assure him. "Your dad runs for town council in a couple of years."

"No kidding!" Ty exclaims. "Does he win?"

I shake my head. "Sorry. But don't tell him. If he

doesn't run, it could change the future."

"Don't worry. How could I explain how I know?"

I don't mention that we're both on the verge of losing the greatest friendship in human history.

"Sorry about the other day," Ty says. "My basement?"

"No problem," I reply, and really mean it. "Let's face it—this is so weird. For all our talk about time travel, who would have believed that one of us would actually do it? You have to at least half think I've gone bananas. I half think I'm bananas myself."

He looks relieved and sticks out his fist for our secret handshake.

As we begin to tap and bump, top and bottom, side and side, he pulls back suddenly.

"That's wrong!" he exclaims. "It's left first, then right, *then* the pinky thing."

I laugh nervously. "I'm a little out of practice. It's been five years."

His eyes narrow. "You mean we don't do the handshake anymore?"

I'm beating myself up inside. How could I be so careless? Of course a smart guy like Ty would instantly see what that means!

I hem and haw. "Well, we're both older—"

"When do we stop?" he presses.

"It just kind of tapers off . . ." I hope I'm not babbling.

"When?" he demands, frowning in full nose wrinkle. "Eighth grade? High school?"

And then I have the perfect answer. "Ava thinks it's babyish."

That shuts him down in a heartbeat. I've found his weak spot. I recognize it, because it used to be my weak spot too.

"This is just between you and me, right?" I remind him. "Nobody else knows about it."

He shrugs. "Who could I tell? They'd think I'm losing it!"

It shows how much things have changed already. There was a time when Ty and I kept each other's secrets out of loyalty to one another. Now it's just because who would believe us?

How sad is that?

TWELVE YEARS OLD
OCTOBER 25

Still no progress tracking down Madame Zeynab. I've been trying that number for Rappaport Holdings at least three times a day. The only answer I ever get is the voice-mail greeting from that Zelda person, who never calls me back, even though I've been leaving dozens of messages. You'd think she'd want to talk to me, if only to tell me to stop calling.

My real fear is that no one ever checks that voice

mail, and I've been talking to dead air. But I'm not giving up, because Madame Zeynab is my only lead.

I've already got my phone out as I enter the house on Wednesday afternoon. I'll call again as soon as I'm done being attacked by Rufus. Every day when I get back from school, I open the door and he throws himself at me, delirious with joy, like he hasn't seen me in years. I don't mind. Six weeks ago, when I came home from the sleepover and found Rufus still alive, I was more delirious than he'll ever be. If I had a tail, it would have been wagging at Rufus speed.

But today, nothing. No window-rattling barks; no bone-crushing body slam, no mouthful of fur. No Rufus.

"Rufus!" I call. "Where are you? It's me!"

I wait for the splash of a shaggy head withdrawing itself from the toilet bowl into a good shake. It doesn't come. No clicking of toenails on tile.

I look in all his familiar haunts—the closets, the pantries, the storage unit where Mom hides the dog food. From the upstairs bedrooms, I check out the front, back, and side yards. I even go into the garage and run the Shop-Vac. That noise is guaranteed to bring Rufus running from any distance up to half a mile. It's his favorite thing in the world. Not this time.

At this point, I'm struggling to contain my panic. Oh, sure, I know that the first time around, Rufus didn't get killed until the end of my sophomore year in high school. But I've proven more than once that things can happen differently in this timeline. Like me playing football. Or building an infinity mirror with Clarisse. Or having plans with my teammates on Saturday night instead of going to Harvest Festival. Rufus dying earlier could be one of those differences. It could even be happening today!

I grab a leash and fly out of the garage. I may be the slowest guy on the Panthers, but I could beat Usain Bolt in a footrace right now. I pound along the sidewalk, bellowing, *"Rufus! . . . Rufus! . . ."*

I'm running full tilt when I almost plow into Ava.

"Mason—what's wrong?"

"My dog is missing!" I rasp.

"Take it easy," she soothes. "You'll get him back."

"You don't understand!" I wail. "He's going to get hit by a Roto-Rooter truck!"

"How could you know something like that?"

"I just do!"

"You're upset. I get that," she says. "I'll help you find

him. A big fluffy sheepdog, right?"

I struggle for calm. "A hundred and twenty pounds, real ugly, and not too bright! And he's got a thing for Roto-Rooter trucks!"

So the two of us jog through the neighborhood, howling *"Rufus!"* and getting not so much as a woof in answer. As frantic as I am about my dog, it occurs to me that, no matter how hard I try to avoid Ava, I seem to be doomed to meet her at every turn. But I can't worry about that now. I need all the help I can get to find Rufus.

We're past the school, still running, still yelling, when a small white truck turns the corner and putt-putts by us. When I see the Roto-Rooter logo painted on the side, I freak out. For some reason, I'm positive that this is the truck that's going to get Rufus.

I take off in a wind sprint that would make Coach Gallo proud. "Mister!" I gasp at the open side. *"Drive carefully! Watch out for dogs!"*

He waves at me and pulls away. Near the end of the street, the truck turns left into the parking lot behind the Roto-Rooter office. And there, sitting quietly on the corner in the exact spot where I take him every Saturday morning, is Rufus.

The sheepdog's eyes never leave the fleet of white trucks in the lot. But he's not chasing anything! He's not even moving. He's just observing—exactly the way I showed him.

I'm stunned. For all the things I tried to teach Rufus over the years, this is the only time he's ever learned one of them.

Ava comes up behind me. "Isn't that him over there on the corner?"

"That's him," I tell her in a shaky voice. "That's my Rufus."

Rufus hears my voice and trots over. Is he glad to see me? Maybe. But he's *super*-glad to meet Ava, who he never even knew existed. He licks her hand. He licks her face.

Ava laughs, petting him. "Animals love me."

Sure. Why should they be different from everybody else?

How am I ever going to keep my distance from this girl?

I click the leash onto Rufus's collar.

Ava shoots me a disapproving look. "How could you call this dog ugly? He's adorable! And well-behaved! Look at how he just sat there, watching."

"You know that snout you just kissed?" I can't resist shooting back. "Well, an hour ago, it was probably submerged in our downstairs toilet."

You have to admire Ava. She doesn't spit, or get grossed out, or even flinch. "I was raised on New York City water. It comes through pipes that are almost two hundred years old." Then she asks the question that's always on the tip of her tongue. "So what's the deal with Saturday night? Are you coming to Harvest Festival?"

For once, I have a real answer for her. After talking for days about our "team plan," the Panthers finally have one. Six of us are going bowling. Not because it was the best activity out of all our choices, but because Austin's older brother is on a bowling team. He offered to drive us to the alley in his van, provided "you losers bowl on the opposite side of the lanes and don't try to pretend you know us."

"Can't," I tell her. "It's team bowling night."

Her face falls. "But you can go bowling any night!"

I shake my head. "Saturday's the only night we've got a lift. There's no alley in Pasco, you know. The closest one is twenty minutes away, on Route 34."

She tries another angle. "Bowling doesn't take that

long. Maybe you can finish up and still make it to the festival before closing. At least you'll want to catch the fireworks."

"Oh, I wouldn't count on it. Austin's brother and his friends are really into bowling. Once they start, it's a late-night thing. And we can't leave till they leave."

By the time Ava breaks off and heads home, I'm feeling pretty good about the whole thing. Time travel may be tricky business, but it's hard to see how I can get my picture taken with Ava behind the Tilt-A-Whirl if I'm at a bowling alley out on Route 34.

Dad's already home when I walk in with Rufus. "Good. You found the dog."

I stare at him. "You knew Rufus was missing?"

"He got out when I stopped home at lunch," he explains.

"And you didn't bring him back?"

He shrugs. "I had appointments. Rufus can look after himself. He's not a puppy. You think there's anything out there bigger and scarier than him?"

"Yeah!" I exclaim. "Roto-Rooter trucks, for one!"

My father brays a laugh. "That fur of his has *ruined* a lot of drains, but I can't picture Rufus *fixing* one."

I suddenly see how Mom gets so frustrated with

Dad. I mean, the dog took off and he just went back to work like it didn't matter. I was the one who had to go find him—Ava and me. And what's Dad doing? Cracking jokes!

I mean, Dad didn't *deliberately* let Rufus out. But when he came home to find the dog still AWOL, why didn't he go out looking for him? Why isn't he out there now?

Dad can be so careless and kind of flaky. No wonder Mom—

At the thought of my mother, my anger evaporates. "Listen, Dad—when Mom gets home, Rufus was never missing, okay?"

He shoots me a blank look. "Why?"

That annoys me even more. I'm trying to keep them from getting into arguments, and Dad seems completely clueless that anything's even wrong. He can't know about the awful day—still three years in the future—that Serena and I help him pack up all his stuff and he moves into an apartment a couple of towns over. But surely he's noticed that he and Mom aren't getting along quite as well as they used to.

"So you guys don't get into a fight about it."

He's mystified. "The dog's fine. What's to fight about?"

I can't stay mad at him. He doesn't know about the divorce. Or the truck.

That's a little detail about time travel that won't make it into anybody's science-fair project.

Sometimes knowing what will happen is the hardest part.

TWELVE YEARS OLD
OCTOBER 28

On Saturday—Harvest Festival day—the Pasco Middle School Panthers take our perfect 2–0 record on the road to nearby Midland to face the Hamilton Middle School Bears. They're also 2–0, so in the locker room, Coach Gallo goes on and on about how the winner will have the inside track on first place in our division.

"In other words," the Dominator growls at me, "don't even think about getting into *this* game, Spaceman! It's for football players only."

I'm not thinking about getting into this game, because I never think about getting into a game. But I can't help noticing that Coach doesn't stick up for me, or chew Dominic out the way he usually does. Everybody's just that nervous.

Everything about Hamilton is intimidating. They're bigger than we are—some of them bigger than Dominic. They block hard and tackle harder. Their fans are rowdier than ours. Plus, there's only one set of bleachers, so our handful of supporters is outnumbered and overwhelmed by the raucous home crowd.

Even the Bears' field seems like it's designed for maximum pain.

"This AstroTurf is murder," Miggy complains as he jogs to the sidelines. "Every time I hit the ground, I get carpet burn all the way up my arms!"

"You should put a lotion with aloe vera on that when you get home," I advise.

The Dominator is beside himself. "Shut up, Spaceman! We don't need lotion; we need real refs! This is the dirtiest team we've ever played!"

Coach Gallo seems to agree. He's got one of the officials over on the sidelines, and he's giving the guy an earful. "I've seen elbows! I've seen trips! I've seen punches! You know what I haven't seen? *Flags!* How about calling some of those penalties?"

The only thing we get out of that is a team foul for unsportsmanlike conduct. It sets the Bears up for their first touchdown. Before you know it, we're down 8–0.

We strike back, but late in the second quarter, the Bears score again. We head into halftime down 16–6.

It's a pretty subdued scene in our locker room. Our players are beat up and demoralized, grumbling about cheap shots and refs looking the other way on purpose. Even Coach Gallo isn't his usual upbeat self, complaining about our "lack of effort."

I can't keep silent. "The problem isn't lack of effort, Coach! The problem is it's not fair!"

Everybody just stares at me.

"Can't you see?" I exclaim. "Those guys are cheating! And the refs are letting them get away with it! How can you have a fair game without fairness? You can't!"

I'm not sure who's the first Panther to start snickering. Maybe Miggy—he thinks I'm kind of funny. But pretty soon the sporadic chuckles turn into a full laugh, and before you know it, the whole team is having a hoot at my expense.

Even Coach Gallo is smiling as we get called back onto the field. "You're one in a million, Rolle. You're the only kid who could bring our guys out of the dumps."

I would love to be able to say that my halftime hilarity jump-starts the Panthers into high gear, and we pulverize the Bears. No such luck. They're still beating us up with their super-rough play, and the refs are looking the other way. We fight hard, but Hamilton builds on their lead. By the end of the third quarter, we're down 30–14, and none of us are laughing anymore.

That's when I see her. She's in the third row of bleachers, not far from our bench—a middle-aged lady, maybe a teacher. She and the person next to her are holding one of those "defense" signs where one part is a D and the other is a section of picket fence. It's hard to get a good look at her, because most of the time her face is behind the pickets. But I swear I know her from somewhere. The thing is, I don't know anybody from Midland. Why would I recognize this woman?

We're halfway through the fourth quarter when I have the answer. It hits me like a bolt of lightning from above. The Bears score another touchdown, putting the game out of reach. During the celebration, she stands up and throws away the fence part of the sign. The sun strikes her at exactly the right angle and I realize how I know her.

She's Madame Zeynab!

I look again, just to make sure it isn't a trick of the light. It's definitely her! She seems younger than the fortune-teller I remember, and her hair is short and brown instead of longer and gray. But it's the same face—I'd bet my life on it!

From that moment on, I can't keep my eyes on the field. My attention is constantly returning to Madame Zeynab in the stands. What's she doing here? Why is someone with supernatural powers wasting her time at a middle school football game?

Whatever the reason, I can't let myself get distracted. For weeks, I've been leaving pathetic messages on some random voice mail that's probably a wrong number. I've been searching for clues to her whereabouts like my life depends on it—which maybe it does. Now she's right here in front of me. If I don't talk to her now—today—I might never get another chance.

The end of the game gets pretty ugly, with a lot of trash-talking and shoving after the whistle blows. At this point, we're down by a mile, and Coach Gallo has no patience for it. He pulls out Dominic and the other starters, and sends in the backups for the final snaps.

"That includes you, Rolle!" he barks at me.

"No!" I exclaim. How can I keep track of Madame Zeynab from the middle of a football game?

Coach misreads my protest as cowardice. "You don't have to play. Just stand there while the quarterback does his kneel-downs to run out the clock."

So instead of waiting on the sidelines, ready to confront the person I've been combing the world for, I'm on the field when the final whistle sounds. There's a small shoving match between the two teams. And me being the smallest and the weakest, I get stuck right at the center of it, being pushed around by both sides. I actually have to drop to the grass and crawl out of the scrum.

Cleated shoes stomp down on me as I fight my way free and jump to my feet. A horrible sight meets my eyes. The bleachers are emptying. The spectators are heading down the stairs and pouring through the exit to the parking lot. My gaze snaps to the spot where Madame Zeynab was sitting just a few minutes ago. It's empty.

"Madame Zeynab!" I howl, sprinting after the crowd.

While all the other players are heading back to their benches, I'm standing by the gate, peering frantically into faces, yelling her name at the top of my lungs. I get a lot of strange looks for that, let me tell you.

Fan after fan, face after face. Pretty soon everybody's gone. No Madame Zeynab. I've lost her. My one chance to make sense of what's happening to me, and I blew it.

I don't know how I manage to turn around and start for the clubhouse. My helmet suddenly weighs nine thousand pounds. My neck muscles barely have the strength to keep my head from rolling off my shoulders.

Just as the depths of despair are rising to swallow me whole, the door marked LADIES swings open, and out steps Madame Zeynab.

I just about throw myself at her feet. "Madame Zeynab—you have no idea how long I've been trying to find you!"

She frowns at me, her gaze blank. "I don't know who you think I am. My name is Zelda Rappaport. My nephew plays kicker on the Bears."

"Zelda!" That rings a bell with me. "I've been

leaving phone messages on the voice mail for Rappaport Holdings! I got the number from the company that used to rent you your tea shop in Pasco!"

"You've got me mixed up with somebody else," she insists.

I pull off my helmet so she can see my face. "I'm that kid, remember? A bunch of us were goofing around outside your shop, and you pulled me inside!"

I sense a spark of recognition in her eyes, and she relents. "All right, kid, you've got me. I'm Madame Zeynab—at least that used to be my business. I'm not doing it anymore."

"I knew it!" I crow. "Your hair is different, and you look younger, but it's definitely you!"

She's annoyed. "I don't just look younger. I *am* younger. The gray hair's a wig. Nobody trusts a *young* fortune-teller. You've got to be old and wise."

My voice is breathless as I ask her the question I've been silently formulating ever since that day on Main Street. "In your shop, you told me I have two futures. What did you mean by that?"

She shrugs. "How should I know? I met a lot of people in that shop."

I hold out my right hand. "Read my palm again.

Whatever you saw, I'm sure it's still there."

Madame Zeynab looks impatient. "There's nothing in your palm but cleat marks. You know why I said 'two futures'? Because I say that to everybody. It sounds mystical and deep, like I'm in touch with the spirit world and I can look into my crystal ball and know everything that's going to happen. Sometimes, I go into a trance, but I wasn't about to do that for a bunch of middle schoolers who were yanking my chain. I don't have supernatural powers, kid. Or paranormal abilities. I was just trying to make a living."

"No," I barely whisper. Madame Zeynab, a fraud? "That's impossible. You must have sensed something special about me, something different. How did you pick me out of all those kids?"

With a smirk, she reaches out and runs a finger across the brush bristles at the top of my forehead. "You've got that thing with the hair. It's funny looking. Makes you stand out." She adds, not unkindly, "You seem like a nice kid. Sincere. But whatever you're looking for, I'm not the answer. Sorry." And she walks away.

I watch her go, practically choking on my disappointment. Madame Zeynab was my one chance that there could be an explanation for why I've been sent back to my seventh-grade life. Now it's gone. Where does that leave me? Will I ever get back to who I used to be, or is this it?

I droop. How could things be any worse?

"Hey!" comes a belligerent voice from behind me. "What do you want with my aunt?"

TWELVE YEARS OLD

OCTOBER 28

wheel to find myself in the path of the entire Bears football team on their way to the locker room.

"Nothing," I mumble. I'm so down in the dumps that it never even occurs to me to worry about being outnumbered twenty-to-one—at least not until the biggest of them grabs me by the jersey and slams me up against the chain-link fence.

"What's your problem, Pasco boy?" the nephew

breathes right in my face.

"She used to be the fortune-teller in our town—" I try to explain.

I get shouted down by a chorus of voices.

"Liar!"

"You're trying to make beef with our fans!"

"Let's teach him a lesson!"

The big guy is advancing menacingly on me when a flying shoulder slams into his chest. Dominic takes him down in a textbook tackle, the best one he's made all season.

"Nobody touches Spaceman but me!" the Dominator pants.

My mind is whirling as the rest of the Panthers clatter onto the scene and surround me protectively. The two teams square off. For a few scary seconds, it seems like the action on the field is about to be resumed, minus the ball.

That's when Coach Gallo wades into the brewing melee. He's not a quiet guy, but I've never heard him yell that loud. *"Panthers—onto the bus! Bears—scram!"*

It brings some of the Hamilton Middle School parents back from the parking lot and defuses the situation.

His face glowing red, Coach marches us onto the bus, jumps on after us, and glares us into silence. "All right, I want to know who started it, and I want to know now!"

Nobody answers.

Coach's searing gaze falls on Dominic. "It was you, Holyoke, wasn't it? I saw you on the ground with that kid!"

Well, how can I let Dominic take the blame after he rescued me? So I say, "It was me."

The coach's eyes bulge. "*You* started a fight with the entire Bears team?"

There's no way I'll ever be able to explain about Madame Zeynab and her nephew. So I give the only other explanation I can think of. "I know it's not right, but I really hated the way they pushed us around all game. So I instigated—beef."

Miggy slaps my shoulder pad. "Way to stick up for the team, Spaceman!"

"Can it, Vincent!" Coach snaps at Miggy. "Sportsmanship's a part of football too, you know. You can't go around instigating beef"—his lips twitch—"every time you don't like the score! And Rolle, I want fifty—I want ten push-ups out of you when we get back to

Pasco! Now, everybody shut up—and no laughing."

I think his last instruction is aimed at himself, because his face is twisted from the effort to keep from cracking up. To be honest, the whole mood on the bus ride home is a lot lighter now. You'd think we won.

The only person who's miserable is me. It's not the ten push-ups I'm worried about—although fifty would have been a problem, since my record is twelve. But I'm really depressed about Madame Zeynab. I thought she was going to be the answer to everything, and she turned out to be a dead end.

When we get back to Pasco Middle School, the whole team gathers around me and counts while I do my ten push-ups. Every time I squeeze one out, there are high fives and cheers. If the Bears could see us, they'd think all those tackles made us loopy.

"One for good luck!" howls Miggy after I hit ten.

So I manage number eleven. The team deserves it after the way they rescued me.

"I hope you've learned your lesson," Coach mumbles before disappearing into his office in the field house.

It's a weird thing to say to players who are celebrating like they just won the Super Bowl.

I change out of my equipment and escape the locker room as fast as I can.

"Pick you up at seven," Austin calls as I head for home.

On top of everything else, I have to go bowling tonight. I'm so upset that I'd love to find an excuse to stay home. But the whole thing was my idea, so I can't very well bail on everybody. And anyway, I still need a place to be that *isn't* Harvest Festival when the storm hits tonight. If Ava is getting kissed under the Tilt-A-Whirl, it's not going to be by me.

As I walk home, I can't help noticing that there isn't a cloud in the sky. It's hard to believe that a giant gale—high winds, rain, thunder, lightning—is coming to tear up the whole town in just a few hours. I remember this from last time—all the adults demanding how could such violent conditions have come without any warning whatsoever? It's a point of town pride that Harvest Festival always has perfect weather—at least it will be until tonight.

At home, I answer a few questions about how the game went, and Mom spreads lotion on my cleat-stomped hands. Dad had a meeting today, so he wasn't at the Bears game. To be honest, I think my Rolle-family cheering section peaked at the season opener.

Why would they come to watch me play now that they've seen how little I actually do? Or maybe what changed their minds was the idea of what Rufus might do in the house if he's left alone.

It's upstairs in my room, surrounded by my pin collection and my solar system model, that my free-falling mood hits rock bottom. I'm stuck here in seventh grade. Sure, I've been twelve for a month and a half already. But now I have to face the fact that I may never get out—not without waiting *five whole years*. And even that might not work. I could just get into another car wreck and wake up twelve again. For all I know, I'm stuck in a repeating loop—like *Groundhog Day*, only instead of reliving the same twenty-four hours, I'm cursed to relive the half decade between twelve and seventeen forever. I'll never get to vote, or go to college, or be an adult. I'll never get married, or have kids, or grow old. There might be some Mason Rolle, in some timeline, who gets to do those things, but it won't be me. I'll be stuck back here, reexperiencing middle and high school forever.

I lie on my bed, staring at the ceiling, racking my brain, trying to find some tiny flaw in my thinking that would prove this isn't the end of the world. Because Ty and I spent so many hundreds of hours twisting and turning the possibilities of time travel, I already know how hopeless this is.

But I can't call Ty and ask his opinion, because I'm not sure he believes me a hundred percent. Or maybe he does believe, and the problem is just that the whole situation is so weird. Here I am jumping through hoops to keep my distance from Ava, in order to protect my friendship with Ty—and the effect is that Ty and I just aren't that close this time around. It's like I'm trying to save something, but first I have to ruin it. What am I saving in the long run?

Well, at least I won't have to agonize over it much longer. Pretty soon I'll be bowling, and Ava will be Harvest Festivaling, and we'll be twelve miles apart. I'd feel more comfortable if we were half a galaxy apart, like the Romulans and the Klingons who inspired the original non-Ava treaty. But twelve miles should do the job.

I jump in the shower, bang down a quick sandwich, and I'm waiting out front when Austin and his brother pull up in an ancient van.

"Hey, Spaceman," Miggy greets me heartily as I slide the door wide. "Is this a sweet ride or what?"

My teammates are draped in various poses across the exposed metal floor.

"Where are the seats?" I ask in amazement.

"It's a cargo van," Austin tosses over his shoulder from the front. That's easy for him to say. He has a seat. "This is my brother, Troy," he adds, indicating the driver.

Troy Stonehart looks a lot like Austin, only with a scruffy beard that doesn't quite cover his jawline. He's a high school senior, which means he's about as old as I should be. Watching someone my age operate a motor vehicle—even *this* vehicle—creates an ache that I feel to the tips of my toes.

We make a few more stops to pick up some of Troy's bowling buddies. By the time we head out onto Route 34, we're so crowded that I feel like I'm sitting in my own lap. To make matters worse, Troy's friends all brought their own bowling balls, and the round cases are rolling around every time we hit a curve. There are also pairs of bowling shoes, and for some reason, a large grapefruit.

"What's the grapefruit for?" Rolando asks.

"The toilet at Victory Lanes is a bottomless pit," Troy explains with relish. "One time, I dropped a peach down there by mistake. Flush—gone! So next time, we tried it with an avocado. Whoosh! I didn't think it would work last week with the orange, because that sucker was pretty big. But it took it down like a champ."

"So tonight's grapefruit night," I conclude.

"Word," he confirms. "And if that's a go, next week we're cleared for butternut squash."

When we finally get to Victory Lanes, there's a police cruiser at the coffee shop, so we have to lie low for fifteen minutes until the officers drive away. If all eleven of us get out at the same time, we'll look like the clown car at the circus, and the cops will arrest us for overloading the van.

Finally, the coast is clear and we troop over to the bowling alley, only to find it locked up tight. Troy pounds on the glass until the manager comes running over and opens the door.

"Sorry, guys, we're closed."

"Why?" Troy demands.

"Plumbing emergency," the woman explains. "A toilet overflowed and shorted out the electrical. We're in the dark."

"Men's room toilet?" asks one of Troy's friends, holding the baggie with the grapefruit behind him and out of sight.

She nods. "And you wouldn't believe what the plumber found in the pipes. The electrician can't get here till Monday. Try back that night."

"Maybe it was the butternut squash," Austin suggests once the manager is gone again.

His brother slaps him in the side of the head. "The butternut squash was for next week! Pay attention!"

"Well, that stinks," comments the grapefruit guy. "What do we do now?"

Troy shrugs. "We might as well go to Harvest Festival."

"*No!!!*" They can probably hear me on the Klingon home world.

"Spaceman's not a big Harvest Festival fan," Austin explains to his brother.

"You and me both, kid," Troy tells me. "But bowling's out. What else is there to do?"

"We can still bowl," I argue. "What about Paradise Lanes? That's not much farther than here."

"We're kind of banned from there," Troy admits. "Their plumbing is real delicate. Like it's our fault the town voted against municipal sewers."

"There's no way I can go to Harvest Festival," I say stoutly.

"Come on, Spaceman," Miggy wheedles. "It won't be so bad. You'll be with us."

"I can't do it."

And pretty soon—wouldn't you know it—I'm back in the van on my way to Harvest Festival. What choice do I have? Troy is my ride. If he's going, my only other option is walking twelve miles home on a night when I know that a giant storm is coming.

What am I going to do?

TWELVE YEARS OLD
OCTOBER 28

use the ride to formulate my plan: I'll go to Harvest Festival, but I won't go in. With any luck, Ava won't look out past the gate and see me. Then I'll walk straight home. It's only a mile from the fairgrounds.

Twenty minutes later, the van screeches to a halt in the Harvest Festival parking lot, sending bowling balls, shoes, and the grapefruit bouncing around the interior. I take a pretty good shot in the hip from a Brunswick three-holer, but nothing is going to stand in the way of me putting as much space as possible between me and the Tilt-A-Whirl. The minute the door slides open, I'm out of here. I may be limping, but I'm leaving.

"Whoa, Spaceman!" Miggy grabs my sleeve. "What's your hurry?"

"I'm going home—"

"No, you're not," Miggy cuts me off. "You nagged us all week about doing something as a team."

"We were supposed to go bowling," I argue. "It's not my fault Austin's wing-nut brother flushed a butternut squash—"

"It was a grapefruit!" Austin exclaims.

"It was an *orange*," Troy corrects. "Get your fruit straight. And I don't appreciate being called a wing nut." With that, he hurls the grapefruit across the parking lot, where it explodes against the windshield of an SUV, sending pulp flying in all directions.

By this time, they've dragged me all the way to the front gate.

I pull free and dust myself off. "I'm not going in."

"Come on, Spaceman," Miggy wheedles. "Just one ride. You have to. You're our team beef instigator!"

I take stock. The sky is clear and full of stars, so I've probably got a little bit of time before the storm blows in. The festival is packed, so the odds of running into Ava are pretty low. And, strange as it seems, these football players are my friends. They definitely weren't in my previous trip through middle school. But right now, I'm as much a part of this group as any one of them. They came out tonight because of me. At the very least, I owe them one ride.

"All right," I agree. "Just one."

First, they spend twenty minutes arguing over which ride is worthy of the beef instigator. And of course they choose Blitzkrieg Mountain, which I've never been on, because I'm too chicken, even five years from now. It's a roller coaster, with deep valleys and cardiac hills. But it's also really old, so you feel like it could fly apart at any minute, leaving you up in the air, but not for long. The kind of ride you hear about on the news, after "Freak accident at . . ."

We have to wait in two lines—a short one to buy ride tickets and a longer one in front of Blitzkrieg Mountain. While we're standing there, the guys are taking bets over who's going to be the first to barf. I'm privately sure I've got that one locked up, but I'm too terrified to open my mouth and place a bet on myself.

I'm trying to tune out the rattle and creak of the ancient tracks when I spy Clarisse in the midst of a group of track team girls. She's almost hard to recognize. Her face is flushed and happy as she munches on a cone of cotton candy. She's laughing—Clarisse doesn't laugh! She moves with confidence. She *belongs* and she knows it. She's like a whole new person. It has nothing to do with being a star athlete. But somehow, along that track, she just sort of found herself. I like to think I had something to do with that, but it was ninety-nine percent her. Good things happen when you get out of your comfort zone and try stuff.

I can almost feel the pat on the back I deserve—except it turns out to be Miggy punching my shoulder. "Hey, Spaceman. We're up next."

As I take my seat on the ride next to Austin and lock down the safety bar, I'm comforted in the knowledge that this version of my Harvest Festival visit is definitely different from last time. There's no way the *old* Mason Rolle would ever be caught dead on Blitzkrieg Mountain.

With a clatter of machinery, the mechanism drags us up to a peak slightly below the ionosphere. There I hang, gazing into the maw of a terrifying drop, when the sound of the motor dies abruptly and the car lurches to a halt.

"What happened?" I wheeze.

Austin looks around in confusion. "I think the ride broke down."

I'm not sure whether to be horrified or relieved. "We're *stuck*? How are we going to get off this thing?"

"No problem," Miggy decides from the seat behind me. "We just have to rock the car until we make it over the top—"

"Don't do that!" I beg, waving my arms at the ride operators below. "See? They're trying to tell us something! Maybe the fire department is coming to—"

Too late. My teammates are shifting their weight forward and back, gradually inching the car over the summit of Blitzkrieg Mountain. When the force of gravity hurls us down the steep track, my stomach leaps up the back of my throat and tickles my molars. We rocket to the bottom at just under the speed of light and shoot three-quarters of the way up the opposite slope. But since the mechanism to carry us over the next hill isn't working anymore, we roll back down again. And up. And down.

"This is *awesome*!" Rolando cheers.

It's a good thing I'm seventeen inside. I don't think twelve-year-old Mason could have handled it. When we finally stop moving at the bottom, a couple of festival employees help us climb out.

I know I'm never going to get a better chance than this. So while everybody's trying to get Austin's silver shark-tooth chain untangled from the safety bar, I sneak off away from the group. The stars are still out, but the breeze is coming up—maybe a little bit more than a breeze. I have to get moving if I'm going to beat the storm.

By now, the festival is so crowded that it's hard to move on the fairgrounds—you have to pick your way through the obstacle course of people. I'm about halfway to the gate when I spot Ty waiting in line at the souvlaki stand.

I'm thrown. Ty wasn't at Harvest Festival the first time I lived this. That was Ava's whole plan back then—to make sure I was there and he wasn't. But things are a little bit different in this timeline.

Ty spies me. "I thought you were bowling with the team."

"It's a long story," I tell him. "Hey, is Ava with you?"

"We're meeting up later for the fireworks," he explains.

"Listen, Ty, there's a big storm coming. You and Ava should probably get home."

He glances up at the starry sky. "What storm?"

I lower my voice. "Remember how I knew about

Ms. Alexander and Mr. Nekomis? That's how I know there's a storm coming tonight. Take my word for it. There won't be any fireworks—not unless you count the lightning."

I can see in his eyes that he doesn't believe me. He's only ever half believed me, and I can't really blame him. It sounds pretty far-fetched and, after all, the Nekomis thing could have been a lucky guess.

I point to the western sky. "There are no stars over there anymore. That's the storm cloud rolling in."

He's stubborn. "I don't see any storm cloud."

It dawns on me then that I'm never going to convince the guy. I've got to get myself out of here. Storm coming in; Ava somewhere in the crowd—the past is setting itself up again. I can smell it. I'm not going to let it happen—as much for Ty's sake as my own.

I give it one last try. "Find Ava and go home!" And I melt away into the crowd and push for the exit.

The breeze is getting stiff and I can hear the first rumbles of thunder—something I don't remember from last time. Of course, I'm listening for it now. Nobody else seems to notice over the hubbub of the crowd and the loud carnival music coming from every ride and food stand.

Next comes a gust that almost knocks me off my

feet, and I grab hold of a post to steady myself until the wind dies down. It doesn't. It grows in intensity, sending clouds of dust and debris swirling in the air.

The crowd notices now, that's for sure. Surprised exclamations raise the noise level, and people grab each other for support and chase flying hats. What's going on? Everybody knows the weather is always perfect for Harvest Festival!

That's when it happens. A blinding flash lights up the night, followed instantly by a tremendous clap of thunder. A jagged fork of lightning arcs across the sky, drawn, as if by an evil spirit, to the transformer just inside the main gate.

POW!!!

The transformer goes up, exactly like I remember it. People absolutely freak, screaming as they raise their arms to try to protect themselves from the rain of sparks. It's an eerie sight—hundreds of hands in the air—but only for a split second. With the transformer blown, the power goes out, and the festival is plunged into darkness. At the same instant, all that music dies. Terrified cries ring out. The crowd tries to move away from the danger, but with so many people in each other's way, it's impossible to get anywhere.

Then the rain sweeps in, sheets of water driven by

the gale-force winds. In the space of a few seconds, I'm as wet as if I've fallen into a swimming pool. At that point, the panic reaches its peak. The crowd scatters. Parents pull toddlers out of strollers and run for cover. Frantic cries for help come from stalled rides all around the midway.

I make a break for the main gate and find a drenched police officer blocking my way. "Back off, kid! This area's closed! There are wires down!"

Behind him, I can see the downed transformer tower, the coils still burning in spite of the rain, cables blowing in the howling wind.

"But there's no power in the wires!" I protest.

"You want to take that chance?"

"How am I supposed to get home?" I demand.

"Use the south exit!" he bawls. "And watch where you step—there's debris all over the place!"

I wheel around and sprint for the other side of the fairgrounds, my sneakers splashing in deep puddles. The south gate is at least a quarter mile away, but what choice do I have? I need to be *gone*.

It's tough going, because I have to slalom around people who are running in every direction imaginable as the chaos blossoms and the clouds continue to dump on us.

Something hits me full in the face, and I very nearly go down on the muddy grass. The impact inkblots the edge of my vision as I stare down at a pink teddy bear. *The* teddy bear—the one that blew into the back of my head five years ago during the same storm on the same night. Last time it struck me from behind, but tonight I'm running in the opposite direction.

It's happening again, almost as if fate knows what it has in mind for me!

Running people jostle me, and I scramble behind a food tent to get away from them. My foot sinks into something soft, and I slide halfway to a full split before regaining my balance. I glance down. Mud? No—hot dog buns, soaked to mush by the rain.

Hot dog buns? But that means I'm —

An all-too-familiar voice calls, "Mason?"

TWELVE YEARS OLD
OCTOBER 28

I look around wildly. There's the back of the Tilt-A-Whirl. I can see the sign blowing wildly and dangerously in the wind. And beneath it, Ava, drenched and shivering.

Get out! I tell myself. *You can pretend you didn't see her in all the darkness and confusion. It's not too late to make this un-happen!*

I spin on a dime and start my retreat.

"Mason, it's me!"

I know it's you! I shout inwardly. *Why do you think I'm running away?*

"Mason!" She calls my name one more time.

I make a fatal mistake. I glance back.

Ava has moved forward, waving her arms to catch my attention. Now she's stopped—*exactly where the giant Tilt-A-Whirl sign is about to come down!*

I don't even think. With a cry of *"No-o-o!"* I close the distance between us, just as the heavy display begins to topple. I clamp both arms around her, tackling style, and hurl the two of us as far as I can, praying it's far enough.

The sign crashes to earth, missing us by inches, and spraying us with broken glass from its light bulbs. Terrified, Ava clings to me.

There's a flash, shorter and dimmer than the lightning. A camera!

Someone took a picture—*the* picture! There was no kiss this time, but it's going to look just as bad on the seventh-grade chat!

I jump back from Ava as if her body has delivered a jarring electric shock. Desperately, I scan the area for the phantom photographer. The first time this happened, I never figured out who it was. Who took the picture that cost me my best friend? Whoever it was set in motion five years of events, leading up to my expulsion from school and a car accident that sent me hurtling back through time to live it over again.

There's nobody around. All the action is taking place on the main midway—the running, the shoving, the screaming. Here behind the scenes, it's just Ava and me.

Then—off to my left—I catch a hint of movement. The faintest glow—a phone screen!

"Hey!" I dash toward it. "Hey, you!"

I come up on a large figure. *Dominic.*

I should have known. Who better to ruin my life than the guy who's been making it miserable since we were in kindergarten together?

Well, here is where it stops! I'm not going to let him do it again!

"Give me your phone, Dominic," I say, strangely calm under the circumstances.

"Spaceman?" His eyes fix on me in the darkness. "Aren't you supposed to be bowling? What happened—you drop a ball on your big brain?"

"I need your phone," I repeat.

"In your dreams!" he sneers.

"I'm not going to wreck it," I persist, my voice steady. "I just have to delete your last picture."

"In your dreams! I got a shot of the Tilt-A-Whirl sign coming down! I can sell it to the *Pasco Post* and get my name in the paper!"

My jaw drops as I realize that Dominic doesn't even know he's got a picture of Ava and me. He was aiming at the sign. He had no clue there was something else going on in the background!

Gradual understanding comes over me as my mind connects the dots. I see Dominic examining his photograph before sending it over to the *Pasco Post*. *Hey, wait*, he asks himself, *who are those two people off in the corner?* He zooms in on his phone—and realizes he has something a lot juicier than a busted sign. And before you know it, Ava and I are the stars of the seventh-grade chat.

That must be how it happened five years ago. And it's about to happen again unless I can get that phone out of Dominic's big paw!

I grab his wrist. It's like holding on to an iron bar.

He doesn't even resist at first. He's too amazed that lowly Spaceman would attempt to muscle him out of something. Angrily, he yanks his hand away, but I stay locked on to his arm. I'm weaker and smaller, but I'm not the pushover he remembers. I've been through a month of football practices, and surely I have the advantage in experience and determination. We may both be twelve-year-olds, but I've lived five years longer than he has. And I'm the only one who understands what's at stake.

"Stop it!" Ava runs up to us. "Stop fighting!"

"Stay out of this!" Dominic and I chorus. It might be the only time we've ever agreed.

But—typical Ava—she doesn't back off. Maybe it's a New York thing. She clamps her own hands onto mine and Dominic's and tries to pull us apart. Pretty soon it's a three-way tug of war, with Dominic's phone as the grand prize.

"Cut—it—out!" Dominic grunts, his voice strained with effort.

With a roar of outrage, Dominic twists his large frame free of Ava and me. As my grip slips, I swipe at the phone in his palm in a last-ditch effort to grab it. I feel my fingers on the case. But my hand is wet—everything's wet. I can't get a firm hold. The phone squirts away from all three of us. It twirls through the air and lands in a muddy puddle in the wet grass.

Dominic dives for it, but I get there first. I rear up my leg and bring my heel down on it with all the desperation and emotion I've been storing up since the last time I lived through this night five years ago.

Water floods in through the shattered screen. The phone flickers once and then dies.

The howl of rage from Dominic drowns out even the chaos of the midway. "You're dead, Spaceman!" He rears back a ham-sized fist and slams it into the side of my head.

The impact has a sledgehammer quality. Ava's scream starts out loud and then fades into echoing silence. I feel myself falling, yet I'm not aware of ever hitting the ground.

SEVENTEEN YEARS OLD

I come to on the wet grass, my cheek throbbing with pain.

"How many fingers?" comes a gruff voice.

I force my eyes open. "Three. Oh, my head!"

"Yeah, it's going to hurt for a while," the man says. "That was a pretty rough tackle."

"No, it wasn't! Dominic punched me!"

"*Me?*" Dominic leans into my field of vision. "I never touched you!"

I notice two things instantly: 1) He's in full football equipment. And 2) he's not the seventh-grade Dominic who just coldcocked me at Harvest Festival. He's *seventeen-year-old* Dominic, high school senior. And that means—

I scramble to my feet and almost keel over from the unfamiliar height. How did I get so tall? The answer is right there, but I don't allow myself to believe it—not until I reach up to my hairline and feel the softness of my famous tuft instead of the brushlike bristles of my twelve-year-old self.

"I'm seventeen again!" I exclaim aloud, mostly to confirm the sound of my older, deeper voice. It's glorious music to my ears.

"What are you talking about, Spaceman?" Miggy sticks his nose in. "You've always been seventeen—ever since you stopped being sixteen!"

I stare at him. He's also in a football uniform. That's when I notice that I'm wearing football gear too. We're standing on the sidelines at Pasco High School's field. And the man with the three fingers is Coach Kovacs of the high school Panthers.

"All right, time-out's over!" Kovacs bawls. "Get in there! Not you, Rolle," he adds to me. "I want the doc to check you out."

"But I don't play football!" I blurt. How do I even begin to describe it? I don't play *high school* football. I played seventh-grade football for a few weeks back in—back in—

When was that? The Bears game was right before the Harvest Festival, and that was—

A few hours ago? Five years ago?

Oh, man, my head hurts!

"What are you talking about Rolle?" Kovacs demands. "You've been playing since middle school. Follow me—I want to get you looked at."

Playing since middle school? I didn't play at all—at least not until I got my second shot at seventh grade. If I'm on the high school team now, does that mean I've been a Panther ever since I was twelve? Why don't I remember all that?

Because you were twelve when you woke up this morning!

The "team doctor" turns out to be Brett Ramirez's mom. As she runs me through the tests to make sure I don't have a concussion, my mind is whirling. First of all, what would this concussion come from? The hit I took on the field that I don't remember? Or the five-years-ago punch in the head from Dominic that I do?

Well, I reason, when I jumped five years *back* in time, I escaped the effects of a pretty bad car accident.

Maybe when I jumped five years *forward*, I got a free pass on the punch.

So if I'm seventeen again, what happened to the accident? I frown. I got into that after learning I was expelled. But I can't be expelled, can I? Nobody plays on Pasco High's sports teams if they don't go to Pasco High, right?

Right?

No car accident, no expulsion, and I'm a varsity high school football player? There's only one possible explanation: Everything has *changed*!

This is huge! I've always believed that if you go back in time and do things differently, you can change the future. But this is proof positive that it actually *works*!

I'm so pumped that I leap up and throw both arms triumphantly into the air, interrupting Dr. Ramirez's concussion test. I pretend it was because of some play on the field.

She favors me with a tolerant smile. "He's fine," she tells Coach Kovacs. "But Mason should sit out the rest of the game. He's done for the day."

The coach doesn't seem devastated by this news. Even on the high school Panthers, I'm the backup to the backup to the backup. A lot is different, but not that.

I'm just settling myself into a comfortable spot on the bench, when an anxious voice behind me rasps, *"Dude—!"*

I wheel to see Ty—seventeen-year-old Ty—his face flushed, breathing hard. I'm instantly on the alert. We're not twelve anymore. *This* Ty and I haven't been friends for five years. And while there was no treaty for me to break this time around, I still ended up in a clinch with Ava underneath the Tilt-A-Whirl on storm night—picture or no.

"Hey, Ty," I begin, my voice cautious. "Let me explain—"

"I ran from row Q," he pants. "That's a lot of butts to climb over. I stepped in this guy's nachos. It got ugly—"

That's already more words than we've exchanged since we were twelve.

He's still babbling. "I saw that hit on the field. Are you okay?"

He stares at me—possibly because he can see how intently I'm staring at him. "I'm good," I manage finally. "Dr. Ramirez gave me the all clear."

He turns his face skyward. "Thank you!"

I can't keep the goofy grin off my face. "We're friends."

He shoots me a look. "You sure you're all right? We've got a big night tonight."

"What's tonight?"

"Aw, man—how hard did that guy hit you? The science fair, Mason. Tonight we present our project!"

"*Our* project?" I echo.

"What's with you, dude?" He's annoyed. "We've only been doing science fairs together since second grade."

"Yeah, bu—" How can I ever explain it?

"Our *time-travel* project!" His voice is getting louder. "I know we've tried the topic before, but this time I think we nailed it!"

One project—my mind is in overdrive trying to sort everything out. So there was no war on the stairs, which explains why I'm not expelled. And since the car accident came while I was driving home from my meeting with Dr. Lalonde, maybe that didn't happen either.

I find Coach Kovacs again. "Listen, Coach, since I'm out of the game anyway, is it okay if I head over to the science fair? Ty and I are presenting tonight."

He barely notices me. "Yeah, sure, kid." He's busy yelling instructions to our quarterback, who turns out to be Austin. The sight of him makes me think of my wild ride bouncing around the back of his brother's van, five years—or just a few hours—ago.

A few teammates high-five me as I exit the sidelines, including Miggy and, amazingly, Dominic.

"Go kick some science-fair butt, Spaceman!" he wishes me.

I'm so surprised to hear a civil word from the Dominator of all people that I blurt, "Sorry for breaking your phone."

He looks shocked. "You broke my phone?"

"You know—when we were twelve," I stammer, embarrassed.

"Oh, that." He grins—maybe the first time I've ever seen him crack a smile that wasn't half sneer. "Your folks made you buy me a new one, remember? I got a nice upgrade out of it."

Wow, if a new phone was all it cost to keep that picture off the seventh-grade chat, then it was the best money I ever spent.

I grab a quick shower and know a brief moment of fear as I'm toweling off. What locker did I use? What if I don't know the combination?

The changing room is open, but it won't look good if I get caught going from locker to locker, rifling through everybody's belongings. I get lucky on the fourth try—I find my Neil deGrasse Tyson T-shirt. I don't recognize the other stuff, but the shirt is definitely mine. Who else on the team would own such a thing? There's a varsity jacket that says *PANTHERS FOOTBALL*, with *ROLLE* stitched under the crest. Definitely me.

Ty is waiting for me, and we make the short walk to the school. Instantly, my eyes are drawn to the parking lot. There it is, in the first row of cars: my Volkswagen Beetle, all in one piece—or at least as much in one piece as it was when I inherited it from Mom. I have to hold myself back from running over there just to touch it, and to run my hands over its beloved rust spots. How would I ever explain *that* to Ty?

The evidence is mounting: no car accident, no expulsion, varsity athlete, friends with Ty. What else is different about my seventeen-year-old life?

We enter the school and head straight for the double gym, where the science fair is housed. I take in row after row of colorful display boards, dioramas, experiments, and working models. This feels more like home than any gridiron, but I remind myself that *this* version of Mason has been playing football since seventh grade and made the varsity team. It's not just the world around me. I'm different too.

"I always love my first view of the science fair," I tell Ty.

He shoots me a strange look. "We were both here yesterday to set it up."

"You know, the whole gym, all filled up," I put in quickly. "Yesterday, there were still a lot of empty tables." It's a guess, but Ty doesn't call me out on it.

I follow him to a large display in the third row. I've never laid eyes on it before, but I'd know it anywhere. It's a perfect combination of the two projects that warred against each other on the stairs in that other life. Mine was Possibilities of Time Travel. His was Time Travel: The Possibilities. This one is titled Time Travel: Infinite Possibilities, and it's a thing of beauty.

I spot elements from both our entries: my International Space Station model, his collectible Buck Rogers action figure. We even decorated part of the background with the spinning-clock wallpaper Ava picked out for the project she did with Ty back in seventh grade.

There's a ton of research. Our booklet is more than three inches thick, and when I leaf through to the end, I wind up at page 214. Single-spaced. I guess that's what you get in a world where Ty and I never become enemies and slice and dice our favorite topic for five extra years.

I can't help noticing a diagram similar to the one from the old Ty-and-Ava project—the one depicting a time traveler, choosing between two paths, A and B. Only in this drawing, every choice leads to other choices, splitting off and branching out until the figure faces an infinite number of futures.

Time Travel: Infinite Possibilities.

"You're right, dude," I breathe. "We finally nailed it."

"I see that your one-track minds are still on the same one track," comes a voice from behind us.

Ms. Alexander steps into our aisle. Wait—she should be Mrs. Nekomis by now. Or did I botch the future so completely that she could be almost anybody?

Ty bails me out. "Hey, Mrs. Nekomis, what do you think?" he asks proudly.

"Excellent work," she approves. "It's a fitting project for a couple of really bright seniors like you two."

I notice that she's missing the bandage across her cheek and the ever-so-slight shiner under her left eye. The rush of relief almost knocks me just as flat as the tackle from the football game. I didn't hurt my favorite teacher. It never happened. No fight on the stairs. No expulsion. It's all coming together.

The main event starts right on time at six. We all get boxed dinners, which we eat in front of our projects. We have to stay put in case the judges have any questions about our work. That's another advantage of time travel as a topic—you don't have to eat a bologna sandwich in front of a white rat who's begrudging you every bite, or a beaker of bubbling chemicals that smell like sewer gas and would send you to the hospital if a tiny splash found its way into your potato chips.

We can tell that the judges are really impressed by our project, because they spend a lot of time asking us questions about our research. Even I manage to sound like I know what I'm talking about—and in a way, I do. Okay, I had nothing to do with this *particular* project. But I'm the one who's actually traveled through time. Most recently, just a couple of hours ago.

We spend quite a while congratulating ourselves after the judges move on. I'm happy to report that I get our secret handshake exactly right without messing it up, like I did that time in my room.

We're pretty excited, almost celebrating, when a peculiar look finds its way onto Ty's face. "Remember that time, back in seventh grade, when you told me you were from the future? What was the deal with that?"

Maybe I owe him the truth, but I just know that if I try to give it to him, it'll only mess us up again. He'll never accept it. I'm not really sure I accept it myself.

So I reply, "All I remember is we weren't getting along. And I thought, what's the topic that always brings us together? Time travel. It was a mistake. I never should have said it."

He nods slowly, taking it in. "You were right, though. Here we are, all these years later, and good old time travel is about to win us another science fair."

The judging takes forever. Eventually, the officials hunker down at the tabulating desk to finalize their results. An excited murmur buzzes around the gym. All eyes are focused on the big screen, where the winning projects will be posted.

We stare. Time Travel: Infinite Possibilities comes in second place.

"Second?" I complain in amazement. "What's the matter with these judges? Like there's anything better in this gym than our entry! What's"—I squint at the big board—"'the Abiotic Synthesis of Organic Compounds'?"

"Dude!" Ty exclaims through lips that can't seem to decide whether to turn down in a scowl or up in a grin. "We just lost to our own girlfriends!"

"Wait—" Suddenly, the results of a science fair mean less than nothing compared with the words that have just come from my best friend's mouth. "We have *girl-friends*?"

31

SEVENTEEN YEARS OLD

A moment later, the answer comes. Ty's girlfriend bursts out of the middle of the crowd and throws her arms around him. They fall into a celebratory embrace, congratulating each other on their one-two finish in the judging.

I blink. I *know* her. That's not exactly right. I *recognize* her. But the Clarisse Ostrov I remember from my other life at seventeen is very different from the smiling girl hugging my best friend. The Coke-bottle glasses have been replaced with sleek, stylish frames. And her gangly, stilt-walker posture has morphed into liquid athletic grace.

I'm blown away. In middle school, Ty didn't even *like* her. My ears are practically still ringing from his marathon gripe session when she joined our astronomy club five years ago. But now that I think about it, there was always a connection between those two. Ty's constant complaining about her meant she was getting under his skin. And as middle school turned to high school, and high school progressed to senior year, that must have blossomed into something more.

"Hey, second place," she greets me playfully. I guess I'm still staring, so she adds, "You're okay with this, right?"

"Of course he is," comes a voice from behind me.

A hand on my shoulder spins me around to face *my* girlfriend.

My heart skips a beat, maybe two. Maybe more. All the accumulated skipped beats of five lost years.

It took half a decade and two different futures, but Ty and I finally know which of us ends up with Ava.

I do.

It sounds impossible, after the effort I put into staying away from her, being mean to her, moving heaven and earth to avoid ending up at Harvest Festival under the Tilt-A-Whirl. But as Ava and I slip into a comfortable embrace, I realize I should have known all along. No matter how hard I tried to keep my distance, fate kept throwing us together. She *chose* me—in two different timelines. She paid five bucks for me when no one else would bid a thin dime. My day as her butler is the best memory of my seventh-grade flashback. When Rufus disappeared, it was Ava who helped me find him. Even the clogged toilet at Victory Lanes was part of the cosmic conspiracy to send me back to Harvest Festival and Ava. What chance did any treaty ever have against that kind of destiny?

"You bet!" I exclaim. "How could Time Travel beat the Abiotic Whatever? Congratulations! You too, Clarisse."

"We always knew we'd edge you guys out one of these years," Ava puts in, exchanging a fist bump with her partner.

"And we had total confidence in you," Ty acknowledges. "In every way except for the part where it actually—you know—happens."

Clarisse fake-punches him in the jaw.

"This is a double celebration for Clarisse," Ty goes on proudly. "Did you guys hear about the track meet?

Her time in the four hundred broke the old county record."

"She's a cheetah," Ava brags. "*And* a tyrant when it comes to science projects."

I remember *that*—even if I got parachuted out of the past before finding out how the judges graded our infinity mirror.

Now that the judging is over, the gym doors are opened and family and friends troop into the science fair. The four of us split up to go find our folks.

Mom, Dad, and Serena are among the early arrivals. The biggest change is in my kid sister. I left her as a nine-year-old fourth grader, and now she's back to the high school freshman I remember. Slowly but surely I'm getting used to the idea that I'm home—not *where* I belong, but *when*. I'm back to my own time.

Mom and Dad look a little older, too, but in their case the change isn't as dramatic. I'm thrilled to see them together, until I get close enough to notice that the wedding rings are missing from their left hands. My father is carrying the keys to the Mustang he bought after he and Mom split up. A lot of things are different in this new timeline, most of them for the better. But all my wheeling and dealing didn't stop the divorce.

I'm disappointed, but in the long run, it's probably

better this way. It shouldn't be up to me to fiddle with the direction two adults choose for their lives. I guess not every path leads to either A or B. Some of them just go to A.

Dad pumps my hand. "Congratulations, kid!"

I shrug. "We didn't win, Dad."

He snorts. "Says who? Some dopey judges? What do they know about time travel?"

"Nothing," I agree. I'm the only one with first-hand experience, but good luck explaining that to the science-fair committee.

"Second place is a lot to be proud of," Mom interjects. "Besides, the girls took the top prize. They must be thrilled!"

We tour the exhibits for a while until the crowd begins to thin. Dad leaves first, and a few minutes later, I head out with my mother and Serena.

No sooner has the toe of my right sneaker hit the pavement of the parking lot than I hear a very familiar bark. From the partly open front window of the van Mom got when I inherited the Volkswagen, a huge fluffy head appears.

"Rufus!" I breathe, trying to keep my voice steady.

"Well, I had to bring him," Mom explains reasonably. "You know what he does to the living room if you leave him alone too long."

I'm practically vibrating in my shoes. It's more than a year *after* the date of the accident with the Roto-Rooter truck, and there's Rufus, alive and well and squeezing himself through the gap in the window. He looks like a giant fluff amoeba, oozing out of the van in slow motion, braying in grievance all the way.

Until this very second, I had no idea which path had been chosen for my dog—life or death. But as he explodes out of the van, drops to the ground, and hurls himself at me, whining and licking, I know that all my Roto-Rooter training paid off. I couldn't do anything about Mom and Dad's divorce. But a lot of other things went my way. And this—Rufus—is the ultimate bonus.

"Your dog isn't too bright," Serena comments as Rufus continues to maul me. "You just left home a few hours ago, and he's acting like he hasn't seen you in, like, five years."

It brings me up short. Just for an instant, I toy with the idea that Rufus might have some kind of insight into the strange journey we've both been on. Oh sure, Rufus hasn't got the brains to figure out what *sit* means. But it's enough to make you wonder how much an English sheepdog can know about time travel.

It takes some doing, but I help Mom and Serena stuff Rufus back into the van. "I'll be right behind you," I promise, and head for the VW on the other side of the parking lot.

It feels funny to get behind the wheel. I've been twelve for a while, so my driving career has been interrupted by my detour through the past.

I inch out onto the street, barely topping ten miles an hour. The last time I piloted this car, I crashed into a furniture van and woke up at a seventh-grade sleepover. That never happened in this timeline—and I want to keep it that way.

I'm stopped at a light when a bright red Ferrari convertible pulls up beside me and guns the engine. I look over to check out who's got a ride like that in a dinky town like Pasco.

My breath catches in my throat. I goggle.

It's none other than Zelda Rappaport—Madame Zeynab. But instead of looking five years older, she seems younger, almost glamorous. She glances at me and winks. Then the light changes, and she disappears with a roar.